A SONG FOR ORPHANS

(A THRONE FOR SISTERS -- BOOK 3)

MORGAN RICE

Books by Morgan Rice

THE WAY OF STEEL
ONLY THE WORTHY (Book #1)

A THRONE FOR SISTERS
A THRONE FOR SISTERS (Book #1)
A COURT FOR THIEVES (Book #2)
A SLONG FOR ORPHANS (Book #3)
A DIRGE FOR PRINCES (Book #4)

OF CROWNS AND GLORY
SLAVE, WARRIOR, QUEEN (Book #1)
ROGUE, PRISONER, PRINCESS (Book #2)
KNIGHT, HEIR, PRINCE (Book #3)
REBEL, PAWN, KING (Book #4)
SOLDIER, BROTHER, SORCERER (Book #5)
HERO, TRAITOR, DAUGHTER (Book #6)
RULER, RIVAL, EXILE (Book #7)
VICTOR, VANQUISHED, SON (Book #8)

KINGS AND SORCERERS
RISE OF THE DRAGONS (Book #1)
RISE OF THE VALIANT (Book #2)
THE WEIGHT OF HONOR (Book #3)
A FORGE OF VALOR (Book #4)
A REALM OF SHADOWS (Book #5)
NIGHT OF THE BOLD (Book #6)

THE SORCERER'S RING
A QUEST OF HEROES (Book #1)
A MARCH OF KINGS (Book #2)
A FATE OF DRAGONS (Book #3)
A CRY OF HONOR (Book #4)
A VOW OF GLORY (Book #5)
A CHARGE OF VALOR (Book #6)
A RITE OF SWORDS (Book #7)
A GRANT OF ARMS (Book #8)
A SKY OF SPELLS (Book #9)
A SEA OF SHIELDS (Book #10)
A REIGN OF STEEL (Book #11)

CHAPTER ONE

Kate stood in front of Siobhan, feeling as nervous as she did before any fight. She should have felt safe; she was standing on the grounds of Thomas's forge, and this woman was supposed to be her teacher.

And yet she felt as though the world was about to disappear from under her.

"Did you hear me?" Siobhan asked. "It is time for you to repay the favor you owe me, apprentice."

The favor that Kate had bargained back at the fountain in exchange for Siobhan's training. The favor that she had been dreading ever since then, because she knew that whatever Siobhan asked, it would be terrible. The woman of the forest was strange and capricious, powerful and dangerous in equal measure. Any task she set would be difficult, and probably unpleasant.

Kate had agreed, though she didn't have a choice.

"What favor?" Kate asked at last. She looked around for Thomas or Will, but it wasn't because she thought the smith or his son could save her from this. Instead, she wanted to make sure that neither of them would find themselves caught up in whatever Siobhan was doing.

The smithy wasn't there, and neither was Will. Instead, she and Siobhan now stood by the fountain of Siobhan's home, the waters running pure for once rather than the stone of it being dry and filled with leaves. Kate knew it had to be an illusion, but when Siobhan stepped up into it, it seemed solid enough. It even dampened the hem of her dress.

"Why so frightened, Kate?" she asked. "I'm only asking you for a favor. Are you afraid that I'll send you to Morgassa to hunt for a roc's egg on the salt plains, or to fight some would-be summoner's creatures in the Far Colonies? I'd have thought you'd enjoy that kind of thing."

"Which is why you won't do it," Kate guessed.

Siobhan quirked a smile at that. "You think I'm cruel, don't you? That I act for no reason? The wind can be cruel if you are standing in it with no coat, and you could no more fathom its reasons than… well, anything I say you cannot do you will take as a challenge, so let's not."

"You're not the wind," Kate pointed out. "The wind can't think, can't feel, can't know wrong from right."

"Oh, is *that* it?" Siobhan said. She sat on the edge of her fountain now. Still, Kate had the impression that if she tried to do the same, she would fall through it and tumble to the grass around Thomas's forge. "You think I'm *evil?*"

Kate didn't want to agree with it, but she couldn't think of a way to disagree without lying. Siobhan might not be able to reach the corners of Kate's mind, any more than Kate's powers could touch Siobhan, but she suspected that the other woman would know if she lied now. She kept silent instead.

"The nuns of your Masked Goddess would have called it evil when you slaughtered them," Siobhan pointed out. "The men of the New Army you butchered would have called you an evil thing, and worse. I'm sure there are a thousand men on Ashton's streets right now who would call you evil, just for being able to read the minds of others."

"Are you trying to tell me that you're good, then?" Kate countered.

Siobhan shrugged at that. "I'm *trying* to tell you the favor you must do. The necessary thing. Because that is what life is, Kate. A succession of necessary things. Do you know the curse of power?"

This sounded a lot like one of Siobhan's lessons. The best Kate could say for it was that at least she wasn't being stabbed in this one.

"No," Kate said. "I don't know the curse of power."

"It's simple," Siobhan said. "If you have power, then everything you do will affect the world. If you have power and you can see what is coming, then even choosing not to act remains a choice. You are responsible for the world just by being in it, and I have been in it a very long time."

"How long?" Kate asked.

Siobhan shook her head. "That is the kind of question whose answer has a price, and you still haven't paid the price for your training, apprentice."

"This favor of yours," Kate said. She was still dreading it, and nothing Siobhan had said made it easier.

"It's a simple enough thing," Siobhan said. "There is someone who must die."

She made it sound as bland as if she were ordering Kate to sweep a floor or fetch water for a bath. She swept a hand around,

2

and the water of the fountain shimmered, showing a young woman walking through a garden. She wore rich fabrics, but none of the insignia of a noble house. A merchant's wife or daughter, then? Someone who had made money another way? She was pleasant looking enough, with a smile at some unheard joke that seemed to take joy in the world.

"Who is this?" Kate asked.

"Her name is Gertrude Illiard," Siobhan said. "She lives in Ashton, in the family compound of her father, the merchant Savis Illiard."

Kate waited for more than that, but there was nothing. Siobhan gave no explanation, no hint as to why this young woman had to die.

"Has she committed some crime?" Kate asked. "Done some terrible thing?"

Siobhan raised an eyebrow. "Do you need to know such a thing to be able to kill? I do not believe that you do."

Kate could feel her anger rising at that. How dare Siobhan ask her to do a thing like this? How *dare* she demand that Kate cover her hands in blood without the slightest reason or explanation?

"I'm not just some killer to send where you want," Kate said.

"Really?" Siobhan stood, pushing off from the lip of the fountain in a movement that was strangely childlike, as if stepping off of a swing, or leaping from the edge of a cart like an urchin who had stolen a ride through the city. "You have killed plenty of times before."

"That's different," Kate insisted.

"Every moment of life is a thing of unique beauty," Siobhan agreed. "But then, every moment is a dull thing, the same as all the others too. You have killed plenty of people, Kate. How is this one so different?"

"They deserved it," Kate said.

"Oh, they deserved it," Siobhan said, and Kate could hear the mockery in her voice even if the shields the other woman always kept in place meant that Kate couldn't see any of the thoughts behind all this. "The nuns deserved it for all they did to you, and the slaver for what he did to your sister?"

"Yes," Kate said. She was certain of that, at least.

"And the boy you killed on the road for daring to come after you?" Siobhan continued. Kate found herself wondering exactly how much the other woman knew. "And the soldiers on the beach for… how did you justify that one, Kate? Was it because they were

3

invading your home, or was it just that your orders had taken you there, and once the fight starts, there isn't time to ask why?"

Kate took a step back from Siobhan, mostly because if Kate hit her, she suspected that there would be consequences that would be too much to deal with.

"Even now," Siobhan said, "I suspect I could put a dozen men or women in front of you through whom you would put a blade willingly. I could find you foe after foe, and you would cut them down. Yet this is different?"

"She's innocent," Kate said.

"As far as you know," Siobhan replied. "Or perhaps I simply haven't told you all the countless deaths she is responsible for. All the misery." Kate blinked, and she was standing on the other side of the fountain. "Or perhaps I simply haven't told you all the good she has done, all the lives she has saved."

"You aren't going to tell me which it is, are you?" Kate asked.

"I have given you a task," Siobhan said. "I expect you to perform it. Your questions and qualms do not come into it. This is about the loyalty an apprentice owes her teacher."

So she wanted to know if Kate would kill just because she had commanded it.

"You could kill this woman yourself, couldn't you?" Kate guessed. "I've seen what you can do, appearing out of nowhere like this. Killing one person, you have the powers to do it."

"And who's to say I'm not doing it?" Siobhan asked. "Perhaps the easiest way for me to do this is to send my apprentice."

"Or perhaps you just want to see what I'll do," Kate guessed. "This is some kind of test."

"Everything is a test, dear," Siobhan said. "Haven't you worked that part out by now? You *will* do this."

What would happen when she did? Would Siobhan even really allow her to kill some stranger? Perhaps that was the game she was playing. Perhaps she intended to allow Kate to go all the way to the edge of murder and then stop her test. Kate hoped that was true, but even so, she didn't like being told what to do like this.

That wasn't a strong enough term for what Kate felt right then. She hated this. She hated Siobhan's constant games, her constant desire to turn her into some kind of tool to use. Running through the forest hunted by ghosts had been bad enough. This was worse.

"What if I say no?" Kate said.

Siobhan's expression darkened.

"Do you think you get to?" she asked. "You are my apprentice, sworn to me. I may do as I wish with you."

Plants sprang up around Kate then, sharp thorns turning them into weapons. They didn't touch her, but the threat was obvious. It seemed that Siobhan wasn't done yet. She gestured over the water of the fountain again, and the scene it showed shifted.

"I could take you and give you over to one of the pleasure gardens of Southern Issettia," Siobhan said. "There is a king there who might be inclined to be cooperative in exchange for the gift."

Kate had a brief glimpse of silk-clad girls running around ahead of a man twice their age.

"I could take you and put you in the slave lines of the Near Colonies," Siobhan continued, gesturing so that the scene showed long lines of workers working with picks and shovels in an open mine. "Perhaps I will tell you where to find the finest stones for merchants who do what I wish."

The scene shifted another time, showing what was obviously a torture chamber. Men and women screamed as masked figures worked with hot irons.

"Or perhaps I will give you to the priests of the Masked Goddess, to earn repentance for your crimes."

"You wouldn't," Kate said.

Siobhan reached out, grabbing her so fast that Kate barely had time to think before the other woman was forcing her head down under the water of the fountain. She cried out, but that just meant that she had no time to take a breath as she plunged into it. The cold of the water surrounded her, and though Kate fought, it felt as though her strength had abandoned her in those moments.

"You don't know what I would do, and what I wouldn't," Siobhan said, her voice seeming to come from a long way away. "You think that I think about the world as you do. You think that I will stop short, or be kind, or ignore your *insults*. I could send you to do any of the things I wanted, and you would still be mine. Mine to do with as I wished."

Kate saw things in the water then. She saw screaming figures wracked with agony. She saw a space filled with pain and violence, terror and helplessness. She recognized some of them, because she'd killed them, or their ghosts, at least. She'd seen their images as they'd chased her through the forest. They were warriors who had been sworn to Siobhan.

"They betrayed me," Siobhan said, "and they paid for their betrayal. You *will* keep your word to me, or I will make you into something more useful. Do as I want, or you will join them, and serve me as they do."

She released Kate then, and Kate came up, spluttering as she fought for air. The fountain was gone now, and they were standing in the yard of the smithy once more. Siobhan was a little way from her now, standing as if nothing had happened.

"I want to be your friend, Kate," she said. "You wouldn't want me for an enemy. But I will do what I must."

"What you must?" Kate shot back. "You think that you have to threaten me, or have people killed?"

Siobhan spread her hands. "As I said, it is the curse of the powerful. You have potential to be very useful in what is to come, and I *will* make the most of that."

"I won't do it," Kate said. "I won't kill some girl for no reason."

Kate lashed out then, not physically, but with her powers. She drew her strength together and threw it like a stone at the walls that sat around Siobhan's mind. It bounced off, the power flickering away.

"You don't have the power to fight me," Siobhan said, "and you don't get to make that choice. Let me make this simpler for you."

She gestured, and the fountain appeared again, the waters shifting. This time, when the image settled, she didn't have to ask who she was looking at.

"Sophia?" Kate said. "Leave her alone, Siobhan, I'm warning you—"

Siobhan grabbed her again, forcing her to look at that image with the awful strength she seemed to possess here.

"Someone is going to die," Siobhan said. "You can choose who, simply by choosing whether you kill Gertrude Illiard. You can kill her, or your sister can die. It is your choice."

Kate stared at her. She knew that it wasn't a choice, not really. Not when it came to her sister. "All right," she said. "I'll do it. I'll do what you want."

She turned, heading for Ashton. She didn't go to say goodbye to Will, Thomas, or Winifred, partly because she didn't want to risk bringing Siobhan that close to them, and partly because she was sure that they would somehow see what it was she had to do next, and they would be ashamed of her for it.

Kate was ashamed. She hated the thought of what she was about to do, and the fact that she had so little choice in it. She just had to hope that it was all a test, and that Siobhan would stop her in time.

6

"I have to do this," she said to herself as she walked. "I have to."

Yes, Siobhan's voice whispered to her, *you do.*

CHAPTER TWO

Sophia walked back toward the camp she'd made with the others, not knowing what to do, what to think, even what to feel. She had to concentrate on every step in the dark, but the truth was that she couldn't concentrate, not after everything she'd just found out. She stumbled over roots, holding onto trees for support as she tried to make sense of the news. She felt leaves tangle in her long red hair, bark brushing stripes of moss against her dress.

Sienne's presence steadied her. The forest cat pushed against her legs, guiding the way back to the spot where the wagon stood, the circle of light from the campfire seeming like the only point of safety in a world that suddenly had no foundations. Cora and Emeline were there, the former indentured servant at the palace and the waif with a talent for touching minds looking at Sophia as if she'd turned into a ghost.

Right then, Sophia wasn't sure she hadn't. She felt insubstantial; unreal, as though the least breath of air might blow her in a dozen different directions, never to fit back together again. Sophia knew the trip back through the trees would have left her looking like a wild thing. She sat against one of the wheels of the wagon, staring blankly ahead while Sienne curled up against her, almost the way a domestic cat would have rather than the large predator she was.

"What is it?" Emeline asked. *Did something happen?* she added mentally.

Cora went to her too, reaching out to touch Sophia's shoulder. "Is something wrong?"

"I…" Sophia laughed, even though laughing was *anything* but the appropriate response to what she was feeling. "I think I'm pregnant."

Somewhere in the middle of saying it, the laughter turned into tears, and once they started, Sophia couldn't stop them. They just poured from her, and even she couldn't tell whether they were tears of happiness or despair, tension at the thought of everything that might be coming for her or something else entirely.

The others moved in to hold her, wrapping their arms around Sophia while the world blurred through the haze of it all.

"It will be all right," Cora said. "We'll make it all work."

Sophia couldn't see how any of it could work right then.

"Sebastian is the father?" Emeline asked.

Sophia nodded. How could she think that there had been anyone else? Then she realized… Emeline was thinking of Rupert, asking if his attempt at rape had gone further than they thought.

"Sebastian…" Sophia managed. "He's the only one I've ever slept with. It's his child."

Their child. Or it would be, in time.

"What are you going to do?" Cora asked.

That was the question to which Sophia didn't have an answer. It was the question that threatened to overwhelm her once again, and that seemed to bring tears just in trying to contemplate it. She couldn't imagine what came next. She couldn't begin to try to figure out how things would work.

Even so, she did her best to think about it. In an ideal world, she and Sebastian would have been married by now, and she would have found out that she was pregnant surrounded by people who would help her, in a warm, safe home where Sophia could bring a child up well.

Instead, she was out in the cold and the wet, learning the news with only Cora and Emeline to tell about it, without even her sister to help her.

Kate? she sent out into the dark. *Can you hear me?*

There was no answer. Perhaps it was the distance that did it, or perhaps Kate was too busy to answer. Perhaps any one of a dozen other things applied, because the truth was that Sophia didn't know enough about the talent she and her sister had to know for sure what could limit it. All she knew was that the darkness swallowed her words as surely as if she had simply yelled them.

"Maybe Sebastian will come for you," Cora said.

Emeline looked at her with incredulity. "Do you really think that will happen? That a prince will come after some girl he's gotten pregnant? That he will even care?"

"Sebastian isn't like most of them in the palace," Sophia said. "He's kind. He's a good man. He—"

"He made you leave," Emeline pointed out.

Sophia couldn't argue with that. Sebastian didn't really have a choice when he'd found out about the ways she'd lied to him, but he *could* have tried to find a way around the objections his family would have raised, or he could have come after her.

9

It was good to think that he might be trying to follow her, but how likely was it really? How realistic was it to hope that he might set off across the country after someone who had deceived him about everything, even down to who she was? Did she think that this was some song, where the gallant prince set off over hill and vale in an effort to find his lady love? It wasn't how things worked. History was full of royal bastards, so what would one more matter?

"You're right," she said. "I can't count on him following. His family wouldn't allow it, even if he was going to do it. But I have to hope, because without Sebastian... I don't think I can do this without him."

"There are people who raise children alone," Emeline said.

There were, but could Sophia be one of them? She knew that she could never, *ever* give a child away to an orphanage after all that she'd been through in the House of the Unclaimed. Yet how could she hope to raise a child when she couldn't even find a place for herself to be safe?

Perhaps there were answers ahead for that part of things as well. The grand house wasn't visible now in the dark, but Sophia knew it was out there, pulling her on with the promise of its secrets. It was the place where her parents had lived, and the place whose corridors still haunted her dreams with half-remembered flames.

She was going there to try to find the truth about who she was and where she fit into the world. Maybe those answers would give her enough stability to be able to raise her child. Maybe they would give her a place where things would be all right. Maybe she could even call for Kate, telling her sister that she'd found a place for all of them.

"You... have options," Cora said, the hesitation in her voice hinting at what those options might be even before Sophia looked at her thoughts.

"You want me to get rid of my child?" Sophia said. Just the thought of it... she wasn't sure that she could. How could she?

"I want you to do whatever you think is best," Cora said. She reached into a pouch on her belt, next to the ones that held makeup. "This is rakkas powder. Any indentured woman soon learns about it, because she can't say no to her master, and her master's wife doesn't want children who aren't hers."

There was a layer of pain and bitterness there that a part of Sophia wanted to understand. Instinctively, she reached out for Cora's thoughts, finding pain, humiliation, a nobleman who had stumbled into the wrong room at a party.

There are some things even we shouldn't intrude on, Emeline sent across to her. Her expression betrayed no hint of what she felt, but Sophia could feel the disapproval there. *If Cora wants to tell us, she will tell us.*

Sophia knew she was right, but even so, it felt wrong that she couldn't be there for her friend the way Cora had been there for her with Prince Rupert.

You're right, she sent back, *I'm sorry.*

Just don't let Cora know that you were prying. With something like this, you know how personal it can be.

Sophia knew, because when it came to Rupert's attempt to force her to be his mistress, it was something she didn't want to talk about, or think about, or have to deal with again in any way.

When it came to the pregnancy, though, it was a different thing. That was about her and Sebastian, and *that* was something big, complicated, and potentially wonderful. It was just that it was also a potential disaster, for her and everyone around her.

"You put it in water," Cora said, explaining the powder, "then drink it. In the morning, you won't be pregnant anymore."

She made it sound so simple as she passed it to Sophia. Even so, Sophia hesitated to take the powder from her. She reached out, and just touching it felt like a betrayal of something between her and Sebastian. She took it from Cora anyway, feeling the weight of the pouch in her hand, staring at it as if that would somehow give her the answers she needed.

"You don't have to," Emeline said. "Maybe you're right. Maybe this prince of yours will come. Or maybe you'll find another way."

"Maybe," Sophia said. She didn't know what to think right then. The idea that she would have a child with Sebastian might be a wonderful thing under other circumstances, might fill her with the joyous prospect of raising a family, settling down, being safe. Here, though, it felt like a challenge that was at least as great as anything they'd faced on the way north. She wasn't sure it was a challenge she could meet.

Where could she raise a child? It wasn't as though she had anywhere to live. She didn't even have a tent of her own at the moment, just the partial shelter of the wagon to keep off the fine drizzle that fell in the darkness and dampened Sophia's hair. They'd even stolen the wagon, so they had to feel a little guilty every time they ate or drank because of how they'd acquired it. Could Sophia spend her whole life stealing? Could she do it while she raised her child?

11

Maybe she would make it to the grand home in the heart of Monthys, and which lay just ahead. What then? It would be ruins, unfit for any human habitation, let alone a safe place in which to bring up a child. Either that, or there would be people already there, and it would take everything Sophia had just to prove who she was to them.

Even after that, then what? Did she think people would just accept a girl with the mask of the goddess tattooed on her calf to show that she was one of the Unclaimed? Did she think people would take her in, give her a space in which to raise her child, or help her in any way? It wasn't what people did with the likes of her.

Could she bring a child into a world like that? Was it right to bring something so helpless as a child into a world that had such cruelty in it? It wasn't as though Sophia knew anything about being a mother, or had anything useful to teach her offspring. Everything she'd learned as a child had been about the cruelty that came from disobedience, or the violence that it was only right for something as wicked as an orphan to expect.

"We don't have to make any decisions now," Emeline said. "This can wait until tomorrow."

Cora shook her head. "The longer you wait, the harder it will be. It's better if—"

"Stop," Sophia said, cutting the potential argument short. "No more talking. I know you're both trying to help, but this isn't something you can decide for me. It's not even something I'm sure I can decide, but I'm going to have to, and I have to do it alone."

This was the kind of thing she wished she could talk about with Kate, but there was still no answer when she called into the night with her thoughts. In any case, the truth was that Kate was probably better at problems that involved enemies to fight, or pursuers to escape. This was the kind of thing she hadn't had to face, any more than Sophia had.

Sophia went to the far side of the cart, taking Cora's powder with her. She didn't tell them what she was going to do next, because right then, she wasn't even sure that she knew herself. Sienne got up to follow her, but Sophia pushed the forest cat away with a flicker of thought.

She'd never felt as alone as she did in that moment.

CHAPTER THREE

The last time Angelica had gone to the Dowager's rooms, it had been because she had been summoned. She had been worried enough then. Now, marching in of her own accord, she was terrified, and Angelica hated that. She hated the sense of powerlessness that followed her, even though she was one of the greatest nobles of the kingdom. She could do as she wished with servants, with so-called friends, with half the nobles of the kingdom, but the Dowager could still have her killed.

It was worse that Angelica had given her that power. She'd done it the moment she tried to drug Sebastian. This wasn't a kingdom where the monarch could just snap her fingers and order a death, but with her… there wasn't a jury of noble peers who would call what she'd done anything other than treason, if the Dowager chose to bring it to that.

So she forced herself to pause as she reached the doors to the Dowager's rooms, composing herself. The guards there said nothing, merely waited for Angelica to make her case to go inside. If she'd had more time, Angelica would have sent a servant to request this audience. If she'd had more confidence in her power here, she would have rebuked the men for not showing her the proper deference.

"I need to see her majesty," Angelica said.

"We were not informed that our queen would be seeing anyone," one of the guards said. There was no apology for it, none of the courtesy that Angelica was due. Silently, Angelica resolved to see the man pay for that in time. Perhaps if she could find a way to repost him to the war?

"I didn't know it would be necessary until a little while ago," Angelica said. "Ask her if she will see me, please. It's about her son."

The guard nodded at that, and set off inside. The mention of Sebastian was enough to motivate him even if Angelica's position couldn't. Perhaps he just knew what the Dowager had already made clear to Angelica: that when it came to her sons, there was little she wouldn't do.

It was what gave Angelica hope that this might work, but it was also what made this dangerous. The Dowager might turn and stop Sebastian from leaving, but she might just as easily have Angelica killed for failing to seduce him as well as she'd been told. Keep him happy, the old bat had told her, don't let him think about another woman. It had been obvious enough what she'd meant.

The guard reappeared quickly enough, holding the door open for Angelica to step through. He didn't bow as he should have, or even announce her with her full title.

"Milady d'Angelica," he called out instead.

Then again, what titles did Angelica have that could stand up to a queen's? What power did she possess that didn't pale into insignificance beside that of the woman who stood in the sitting room of her apartments, her face a carefully composed mask.

Angelica curtseyed, because she didn't dare do anything else. The Dowager gestured impatiently for her to stand.

"A sudden visit," she said without a smile, "and news about my son. I think we can dispense with that."

And if Angelica hadn't curtseyed, no doubt Sebastian's mother would have rebuked her for it.

"You told me to bring you any news about Sebastian, Your Majesty," Angelica said.

The Dowager nodded, moving over to a comfortable-looking chair. She didn't offer Angelica a seat.

"I know what I said. I also know what I said would happen if you didn't."

Angelica could remember the threats too. The Mask of Lead, the traditional punishment for traitors. Just the thought of it made her shudder.

"Well?" the Dowager asked. "Have you managed to make my son the happiest husband-to-be in the circle of the world?"

"He says that he is leaving," Angelica said. "He was angry at being manipulated, and he declared that he was going after the whore he loved before."

"And you did nothing to stop him?" the Dowager demanded.

Angelica could hardly believe that. "What would you have had me do? Tackle him at the door? Lock him in his chambers?"

"Do I have to spell it out to you?" the Dowager said. "Sebastian might not be Rupert, but he is still a man."

"You think I didn't try that?" Angelica countered. That part stung worse than the rest of it. No one had rejected her before. Whoever she wanted, whether it was out of genuine desire or simply to prove that she could, had come running. Sebastian had been the only one to ever turn her down. "He's in love."

The Dowager sat there, and seemed to calm a little. "So you're telling me that you can't be the wife I need for my son? That you can't make him happy? That you're useless to me?"

Too late, Angelica saw the danger in it.

"I didn't say that," she said. "I only came because—"

"Because you wanted me to solve your problems for you, and because you were afraid of what would happen if you didn't," the Dowager said. She stood, her finger jabbing at Angelica's chest. "Well, I am prepared to give you one piece of advice. If he is following the girl, the most likely place she will go is Monthys, in the north. There, is that sufficient for you, or do I need to draw you a map?"

"How do you know that?" Angelica asked.

"Because I know what this is all about," the Dowager snapped back. "Let's make it clear, Milady. I have already done something to control my son. I have sent *you* to distract him. Now, if necessary, I will discard that option, but there would be no marriage then, and I would be... very disappointed in you."

She didn't need to spell out the threat. At best, Angelica would find herself sent away from the court. At worst...

"I'll fix this," she promised. "I'll make sure that Sebastian loves me, and only me."

"You do that," the Dowager said. "Whatever it takes, you do that."

***

Angelica had no time for the usual niceties of noble travel. This was not the moment to meander along in a carriage, hemmed in by a gaggle of hangers-on, and surrounded by enough servants to slow her to a walk. Instead, she had her servants dig out riding clothes, and with her own hands she packed a small bag with things she might need. She even tied her hair back in a much simpler style than her usual elaborate braids, knowing that there would be no time for such things on the road. Besides, there were some things it might be better not to be recognized doing.

She set out into Ashton with a cloak around her to make sure no one saw who she was. She took a half mask as well, and in the city, that was a common enough mark of religious fervor that no one questioned it. She rode to the gates of the palace first, stopping by the guards and spinning a coin between her fingers.

"Prince Sebastian," she said. "Which way did he go?"

She knew she couldn't hide her identity from the guards, but probably they wouldn't ask questions either. They would simply assume that she was following after the man she loved and intended to marry. It was even the truth, in its way.

"That way, Milady," one of the men said, pointing. "The way the young women went when they ran from the palace a few days ago."

Angelica should have guessed as much. He pointed, and Angelica went. She followed Sebastian through the city like a hound at the hunt, hoping she could get to him before he went too far. She felt almost like some spirit bound to the city. In her home, she was powerful. She knew the people here, and whom to talk to. The further she went beyond it, the more she would have to rely on her own wits. She asked the same questions Sebastian must have asked as he went, and received the same answers.

She heard about the flight of Sophia and the serving girl through the city from a series of folk so filthy she wouldn't even have noticed them under other circumstances. They remembered it because it had been the most exciting thing to happen in their dreary lives for weeks. Maybe she and Sebastian would become another piece of gossip for them. Angelica hoped not. From a gossiping fishwife who genuflected to her as she passed, Angelica heard about a chase through the city's streets. From an urchin so grubby that she couldn't tell if it was a boy or a girl, she heard about them diving into the barrels of a cart to hide.

"And then the woman with the cart told them to come with her," the filthy creature told her. "They all drove off together."

Angelica tossed it a small coin. "If you're lying to me, I'll see to it that you're thrown from one of the bridges."

Now that she knew about the cart, it was easy to track their progress. They'd headed for the northernmost exit from the city, and that seemed to make it clear where they were heading: Monthys. Angelica sped up, hoping that the Dowager's information was right even as she wondered what the old woman was keeping from her. She didn't like being a pawn in someone else's game. One day, the old hag would pay for it.

For today, she had to get ahead of Sebastian.

Angelica had no thoughts about trying to change his mind, not yet. He would still be burning with the need to find that… that… Angelica couldn't think of words harsh enough for one of the Indentured who pretended to be something she wasn't, who seduced the prince who was meant for Angelica, and who had been nothing but an impediment since she arrived.

She couldn't let Sebastian find her, but he wouldn't simply turn away from the search because she asked. That meant that she needed to act, and act fast, if she was going to make this turn out right.

"Out of the way!" she called, before spurring her horse forward at the kind of speed that promised a crushing fall to anyone stupid enough to stand in its path. She headed out from the city, guessing at the route the wagon must have taken. She cut across the fields, jumping hedges so close that she could feel the brush of the branches against her boots. Anything that would let her get ahead of Sebastian before he went too far.

Eventually, she saw a crossroads ahead, and a man leaning on the signpost there with a flagon of cider in one hand and the air of someone who didn't intend to move.

"You," Angelica said. "Are you here every day? Did you see a cart with three girls pass by here on the way north a few days ago?"

The man hesitated, regarding his drink. "I—"

"It doesn't matter," Angelica said. She hefted a purse, the clink of the Royals inside unmistakable. "You were now. A young man named Sebastian will ask you, and if you want these coins, you will say that you saw them. Three young women, one with red hair, one dressed like a servant from the palace."

"Three young women?" the man said.

"One with red hair," Angelica repeated with what she hoped was a suitable degree of patience. "They asked you the way to Barriston."

It was the wrong way, of course. More than that, it was a journey that would keep Sebastian occupied for a while, and that would cool his foolish desire for Sophia when he failed to find her. It would give him a chance to remember his duty.

"They did all that?" the man asked.

"They did if you want the coin," Angelica snapped back. "Half now, half when it's done. Repeat it to me, so I know you're not too drunk to say it when the time comes."

He managed it, and that was good enough. It had to be. Angelica gave him his coin and rode on, wondering how long it would take him to realize that she wouldn't be coming back with the other half. Hopefully, he wouldn't work it out until well after Sebastian had been by.

For her part, she had to be long gone by that point. She couldn't afford for Sebastian to see her, or he would work out what she'd done. Besides, she needed all the head start that she could get. It was a long way north to Monthys, and Angelica needed to finish everything that she needed to do well before Sebastian realized his mistake and came after her.

"There will be enough time," Angelica reassured herself as she rode north. "I'll get it done, and be back in Ashton before Sebastian realizes that anything's wrong."

Get it done. Such a delicate way of phrasing it, as if she were still in court, feigning shock while setting out the indiscretions of some minor noble girl for the rumor mill to digest. Why not say what she meant? That, once she found Sophia, there was only one thing that was going to ensure that she would never interfere with her or Sebastian's life again; only one thing that would make it clear that Sebastian was hers, and that would show the Dowager that Angelica was willing to do whatever was required to secure her position. There was only one thing that was going to leave Angelica feeling safe.

Sophia was going to have to die.

CHAPTER FOUR

Sebastian had no doubt as he rode that there would be trouble for what he was doing now. Riding away like this, against his mother's orders, avoiding the marriage she had set for him? For a noble from another family, it would have been enough to warrant disinheritance. For the son of the Dowager, it was tantamount to treason.

"It won't come to that," Sebastian said as his horse thundered onward. "And even if it does, Sophia is worth it."

He knew what he was giving up by doing this. When he found her, when he married her, they wouldn't just be able to walk back into Ashton in triumph, take up residence in the palace, and assume that everyone would be happy. If they were able to return at all, it would be under a cloud of disgrace.

"I don't care," Sebastian told his horse. Worrying about disgrace and honor had been what had gotten him into this mess in the first place. He'd put Sophia aside because of what he'd assumed people would think about her. He hadn't even made them raise their voices in disapproval; he'd just acted, knowing what they would say.

It had been a weak, cowardly thing to do, and now he was going to undo it, if he could.

Sophia was worth a dozen of the nobles he'd spent his time around growing up. A hundred. It didn't matter if she had the Masked Goddess's mark tattooed on her calf to claim her, she was the only woman Sebastian could even begin to dream of marrying.

Certainly not Milady d'Angelica. She was everything that the court represented: vain, shallow, manipulative, focused on her own wealth and success rather than anyone else. It didn't matter that she was beautiful, or from the right family, that she was intelligent or the sealing of an alliance within the country. She wasn't the woman Sebastian wanted.

"I was still harsh with her when I left," Sebastian said. He wondered what anyone watching would think, with him talking to his horse like this. Yet the truth was that he didn't care now *what* people thought, and in a lot of ways, the horse was a better listener than most of the people around him had been at the palace.

He knew how things worked there. Angelica hadn't been trying to trick him; she'd simply been trying to put something she knew he would find unpleasant in the best way possible. Looked at through the eyes of a world where the two of them had no choice about whom they were married to, it could even be seen as a kindness.

It was just that Sebastian didn't want to think that way anymore.

"I don't want to be stuck in a place where my only duty is to keep breathing in case Rupert dies," he told his horse. "I don't want to be somewhere my value is as breeding stock, or as something to be sold on to promote the right connections."

Looked at like that, the horse probably understood his predicament as well as any noble could. Weren't the finest horses sold on for their breeding potential? Didn't those nobles who liked to race the length of country lanes or ride to the hunt keep records of every line, every foal? Wouldn't every one of them kill their own prize stallions before they allowed a single drop of the wrong blood to enter the bloodlines?

"I'll find her, and I'll find a priest to marry us," Sebastian said. "Even if Mother wants to charge us with treason over it, she'll still need to persuade the Assembly of Nobles."

They wouldn't just kill a prince on a whim. Probably, some of them would be sympathetic, given enough time. Failing that, he and Sophia could always elope into the mountain lands of the north, or slip over the Knifewater together unseen, or even just retire to the lands Sebastian was supposed to be a duke of. They would find a way to make it work.

"I just have to find her first," Sebastian said, as his horse took him out of the city, into the open countryside.

He felt confident that he would catch up to her, even with how far ahead she had to be by now. He'd found people who had seen what had happened when she ran from the palace, asking guards for their reports, then listening to stories from the people of the city. Most of them had been cautious about talking to him, but he'd managed to get enough fragments together to at least get a general sense of the direction Sophia had been moving in.

From what he'd heard, she was in a cart, which meant that she would be moving faster than a walking pace, but nowhere near as fast as Sebastian could move on horseback. He would find a way to catch up to her, even if it meant riding without rest until he did it.

Perhaps that was part of his penance for pushing her out in the first place.

Sebastian pressed forward until he saw the crossroads, finally slowing his horse to a walk as he tried to work out which way to go.

There was a man asleep against the post of the crossroads, a straw hat pulled down over his eyes. A cider jug beside him suggested the reason he was snoring like a donkey. Sebastian let him sleep for now, looking up at the sign. East would lead to the coast, but Sebastian doubted that Sophia had the means to take a ship, or anywhere to go if she did. South would lead back to Ashton, so that was out.

That left the road leading north, and the one leading west. Without any additional information, Sebastian had no idea about which route to take. He could try looking for cart tracks on one of the dirt sections of the road, he guessed, but that implied that he had the skills to know what he was looking for, or to pick out Sophia's cart from the hundreds of others that might have gone past in the days since then.

That left asking for help, and hoping.

Gently, using the toe of his boot, Sebastian nudged the foot of the sleeping man. He stepped back as the man spluttered and came awake, because he didn't know how someone that drunk might react to the sight of him there.

"Whaddizit?" the man managed. He also managed to pull himself up to his feet, which seemed quite impressive under the circumstances. "Who are you? What do you want?"

Even now, he seemed to have to hold onto the post to steady himself. Sebastian was starting to wonder if this was such a good idea.

"Are you here regularly?" he asked. He both needed the answer to be yes and hoped that it would be no, because what would that say about the man's life.

"Why do you want to know?" the drunk shot back.

Sebastian was starting to realize that he wasn't going to find what he wanted here. Even if this man spent most of his time by the crossroads, Sebastian doubted that he would be sober often enough to notice much.

"It doesn't matter," he said. "I was looking for someone who might have come by here, but I doubt you can help me. I'm sorry to have bothered you."

He turned back toward his horse.

"Wait," the man said. "You... you're Sebastian, aren't you?"

Sebastian stopped at the sound of his name, turning back toward the man with a frown.

"How do you know my name?" he asked.

The man staggered a little. "What name?"

"My name," Sebastian said. "You just called me Sebastian."

"Wait, you're Sebastian?"

Sebastian did his best to be patient. This man was obviously looking for him, and Sebastian could only think of a few reasons why that might be the case.

"Yes, I am," he said. "What I want to know is why you're looking for me."

"I was…" The man paused for a moment, his brow crinkling. "I was supposed to give you a message."

"A message?" Sebastian said. It seemed too good to be true, but even so, he dared to hope. "From whom?"

"There was this woman," the drunk said, and that was enough to fan the embers of hope into a fully fledged fire.

"What woman?" Sebastian said.

The other man wasn't looking at him now though. If anything, it looked as though he was half drifting back to sleep. Sebastian caught hold of him, half holding him up, half shaking him awake.

"What woman?" he repeated.

"There was something… a red-haired woman, on a cart."

"That's her!" Sebastian said, his excitement getting the better of him in that moment. "Was this a few days ago?"

The drunk took his time considering it. "I don't know. Could be. What day is it?"

Sebastian ignored that. It was enough that he'd found the clue Sophia had left for him. "The woman… that's Sophia. Where did she go? What was her message?"

He gave the drunk another shake as he started to drift off again, and Sebastian had to admit that it was at least partly from frustration. He needed to know what message Sophia had left with this man.

Why him? Had there been no one else Sophia could leave her message with? Looking at the man he was all but holding up, Sebastian knew the answer to that: she'd been sure that Sebastian would run into him, because she'd guessed that he wouldn't be going anywhere. He'd been the best way to get a message to Sebastian if he followed.

Which meant that she wanted him to follow. She wanted him to be able to find her. Just the thought of it was enough to lift Sebastian's heart, because it meant that Sophia might be prepared to forgive all that he'd done to her. She wouldn't provide him with a way to follow her if she didn't see a way for them to be together again, would she?

"What was the message?" Sebastian repeated.

"She gave me money," the man said. "Said to say that... damn, I know I remembered it..."

"Think," Sebastian said. "It's important."

"She said to tell you that she'd gone off to Barriston!" the drunk said with a note of triumph. "Said to say that I'd seen it with my own eyes."

"Barriston?" Sebastian asked, eyeing the sign at the crossroads. "You're certain?"

The town didn't seem like a place that Sophia had any reason to go to, but maybe that was the point, given that she had been running. It was a provincial kind of town, without the size or the population of Ashton, but it had some wealth thanks to its glove industry. Perhaps it was as good a place as any for Sophia to go.

The other man nodded, and that was enough for Sebastian. If Sophia had left him a message, then it didn't matter who she had chosen to deliver it for her. What mattered was that he'd gotten her message, and he knew which way to go to follow her. As thanks, Sebastian tossed the man by the crossroads a coin from his belt pouch, then rushed to mount his horse.

He steered the creature west, heeling it forward as he set off in the direction of Barriston. It would take time to get there, but he would push as hard as he dared on the way. He would catch up to her there, or maybe he would even overtake her on the road. Either way, he would find her, and they would be together.

"I'm coming, Sophia," he promised, while around him, the landscape of the Ridings sped by. Now that he knew she wanted to be found, he would do anything he had to do to catch up to her.

CHAPTER FIVE

Dowager Queen Mary of the House of Flamberg stood in the middle of her gardens, lifting a white rose to her nose and taking in the delicate scent. She had become good at masking her impatience over the years, and where her eldest son was concerned, impatience was an emotion that came to her far too readily.

"What is this rose?" she asked one of the gardeners.

"A variety created by one of our indentured gardeners," the man said. "She calls it the Bright Star."

"Congratulate her on it and inform her that from now on it will be known as the Dowager's Star," the queen said. It was both a compliment and a reminder to the gardener that those who owned the indentured's debt could do as they wished with her creations. It was the kind of double-sided move the Dowager enjoyed for its efficiency.

She'd become good at making them too. After the civil wars, it would have been so easy to slide into powerlessness. Instead, she'd found the balancing points between the Assembly of Nobles and the Masked Goddess's church, the unwashed masses and the merchants. She'd done it with intelligence, ruthlessness, and patience.

Even patience had its limits, though.

"Before you do that," the Dowager said, "kindly drag my son out of whatever brothel he is ensconced in and remind him that his queen is waiting for him."

The Dowager stood by a sundial, watching the shift of the shadow as she waited for the wastrel who stood as heir to the kingdom. It had moved a full finger's breadth by the time she heard Rupert's footsteps approaching.

"I must be going senile in my old age," the Dowager said, "because I'm obviously misremembering things. The part where I summoned you to me half an hour ago, for example."

"Hello to you too, Mother," Rupert said, not looking contrite in the least.

It would have been better if there were any sense that he had been using his time wisely. Instead, the disheveled state of his

24

clothes said that she'd been right in her earlier guess about where he would be. That, or he'd been hunting. There were so few activities her elder son seemed to actually care about.

"I see that your bruises are finally starting to fade," the Dowager said. "Or have you finally started to get better at covering them with powder?"

She saw her son flush with anger at that, but she didn't care. If he'd thought himself able to lash out at her, he would have done it years ago, but Rupert was good at knowing who he could and couldn't direct his temper at.

"I was caught by surprise," Rupert said.

"By a serving girl," the Dowager replied calmly. "From what I hear, while you were in the middle of attempting to force yourself on your brother's former fiancée."

Rupert stood there open-mouthed for several seconds. Hadn't he learned by now that his mother heard what went on in her kingdom, and in her home? Did he think that one remained the ruler of an island as divided as this one without spies? The Dowager sighed. He really did have too much to learn, and showed no signs of being willing to learn those lessons.

"Sebastian had put her aside by then," he insisted. "She was fair game, and nothing but an indentured whore anyway."

"All those poets who write about you as a golden prince have really never met you, have they?" the Dowager said, although the truth was that she'd paid more than a few to make sure the poems turned out right. A prince should have the reputation he desired, not the one he'd earned. With the right reputation, Rupert might even have the Assembly of Nobles' acclamation when the time came for him to rule. "Did it not occur to you that Sebastian might be angry if he heard what you tried to do?"

Rupert frowned at that, and the Dowager could see that her son didn't understand it.

"Why would he? He wasn't going to marry her, and in any case, I'm the eldest, I'll be his king one day. He wouldn't dare to do anything."

"If you think that," the Dowager said, "you don't know your brother."

Rupert laughed at that. "And *you* know him, Mother? Trying to marry him off? No wonder he ran."

The Dowager bit back her anger.

"Yes, Sebastian ran. I'll admit that I underestimated the strength of his feelings there, but that can be solved."

"By dealing with the girl," Rupert said.

The Dowager nodded. "I assume it's a task you want for yourself?"

"Absolutely."

Rupert didn't even hesitate. The Dowager had never thought that he would. That was good, in its way, because a ruler shouldn't shrink from doing what was necessary, yet she doubted that Rupert was thinking in those terms. He just wanted revenge for the bruises that marred his otherwise perfect features even now.

"Let us be clear," the Dowager said. "It is necessary that this girl should die, both to undo the insult to you, and because of the... difficulties she could represent."

"With a marriage between Sebastian and an unsuitable girl," Rupert said. "How embarrassing."

The Dowager plucked one of the flowers nearby. "Embarrassment is like this rose. It looks innocuous enough. It draws the eye. Yet it still has cutting thorns. Our power is an illusion, kept alive because people believe in us. If they embarrass us, that faith could falter." She closed her hand, ignoring the pain as she crushed it. "These things must be dealt with, whatever the cost."

It was better to let Rupert think that this was about maintaining the prestige of their family. It was better than acknowledging the real danger the girl represented. When the Dowager had realized who she really was... well, the world had turned into a crystal-sharp thing, clear and full of cutting edges. She could *not* allow that danger to continue.

"I'll kill her," Rupert said.

"Quietly," the Dowager added. "Without fuss. I don't want you creating more trouble than you solve."

"I will deal with it," Rupert insisted.

The Dowager wasn't sure if he would, but she had other pieces in play when it came to the girl. The trick was to only use the ones who had their own reasons to act. Give commands, and she would simply draw attention to the fact that this girl was someone worth watching.

It had taken all her strength of will not to react the first time she had seen Sophia, at dinner. Not to betray what she felt at the sight of that face, or at the news that Sebastian planned to *marry* her.

That her younger son had left in pursuit of her made things more complicated. Ordinarily, Sebastian was the stable one, the clever one, the dutiful one. In a lot of ways, he would make a better king than his brother, but that wasn't the way these things worked. No, his role was to live his life quietly, doing as he was commanded, *not* to run off, doing what he wished.

"I have another thing for you to do as well," the Dowager said. She set off on a slow circuit of the garden, forcing Rupert to follow after her the way a dog followed after its master. In this case, though, Rupert was a hunting dog, and she was about to provide the scent.

"Haven't you given me enough tasks, Mother?" he demanded. Sebastian wouldn't have argued. *Hadn't* argued with anything, except on the one matter where it counted.

"You cause less trouble when you're busy," the Dowager said. "In any case, this is the kind of task where your presence might actually be useful. Your brother has acted out of emotion, running off like this. I think it will take a brother's touch to bring him back."

Rupert laughed at that. "Judging by the way he set off, it will take a regiment to bring him back."

"Then *take one*," the Dowager snapped back. "You have a commission, so use it. Take the men you need. Find your brother and bring him back."

"In pristine condition, no doubt?" Rupert said.

The Dowager's eyes narrowed at that. "He is your *brother*, Rupert. You will not hurt him any more than is necessary to bring him home safely."

Rupert looked down. "Of course, Mother. While I'm at all this, would you like me to do a third thing?"

There was something about the way he said it that made the Dowager pause, turning to face her son.

"What did you have in mind?" she asked.

Rupert smiled and waved a hand. From the far end of the garden, a figure in the robes of a priest started to approach. When he got within a few paces, he swept into a deep bow.

"Mother," Rupert said, "may I introduce Kirkus, second secretary to the high priestess of the Masked Goddess?"

"Justina sent you?" the Dowager asked, deliberately using the high priestess's name to remind the man of the company he was now in.

"No, your majesty," the priest said, "but there is a matter of the utmost importance."

The Dowager sighed at that. In her experience, matters of the utmost importance to priests mostly involved donations to their temples, the need to punish the sinful who apparently weren't being sufficiently afflicted by the law, or requests to interfere in the affairs of their brethren across the Knifewater. Justina had learned to keep those matters to herself, but her underlings sometimes buzzed around, irritating her like black-clad wasps.

"He's worth listening to, Mother," Rupert said. "He's been spending his time around the court, trying to gain an audience. You asked where I was before? I was finding Kirkus here, because I guessed that you might want to hear what he had to say."

That was enough to make the Dowager reconsider the priest. Anything that was enough to make Rupert pull his mind away from the women of the court was worthy of her attention, at least for a short while.

"Very well," she said. "What do you have to say, second secretary?"

"Your Majesty," the man said, "there has been a most callous assault on our House of the Unclaimed, and then on the rights of the priesthood."

"You think I haven't heard about it?" the Dowager countered. She looked over to Rupert. "This is your news?"

"Your majesty," the priest insisted, "the girl who killed our nuns suffered no justice. Instead, she found sanctuary in one of the Free Companies. With Lord Cranston's men."

The name of the company caught the Dowager's interest, a little.

"Lord Cranston's company has been most helpful in the recent past," the Dowager said. "They assisted in fighting off a force of raiders from our shores."

"Does that—"

"Be silent," the Dowager snapped, cutting the man off in mid-rebuttal. "If Justina really cared about this, she would raise the issue. Rupert, why have you brought this to me?"

Her son smiled like a shark. "Because I have been asking questions, Mother. I have been very thorough."

Meaning that he tortured someone. Was it really the only way her son knew to do things?

"I believe the girl Kirkus seeks to be the sister of Sophia," Rupert said. "Some of the survivors from the House of the Unclaimed spoke about two sisters, one of whom was trying to save the other."

Two sisters. The Dowager swallowed. Yes, that would fit, wouldn't it? Her information had concentrated on Sophia, but if the other was alive as well, then she could be just as much of a danger. Perhaps more, judging by what she'd managed to do so far.

"Thank you, Kirkus," she managed. "I will deal with this situation. Please leave me to discuss it with my son."

She managed to turn it into a dismissal, and the man hurried from her sight. She tried to think this through. It was obvious what

28

needed to happen next. The question was simply how. She thought for a moment… yes, that might work.

"So," Rupert said, "do you want me to kill this sister of hers as well? I take it we don't want something like *that* seeking revenge?"

Of course he would think it was about that. He didn't know the real danger they represented, or the problems that could result if anyone found out the truth.

"What do you propose to do?" the Dowager said. "March in and take on Peter Cranston's regiment? I'm likely to lose a son if you do that, Rupert."

"You think I couldn't beat them?" he shot back.

The Dowager waved that away. "I think there's an easier way. The New Army is gathering, so we will send Lord Cranston's regiment against them. If I choose the battle wisely, our enemies will be harmed, while the girl will die, and it will look like no more than another unmarked grave in a war."

Rupert looked at her then with a kind of admiration. "Why, Mother, I never knew that you could be so cold-blooded."

No, he didn't, because he hadn't seen the things she'd done to keep the scraps of her power she had. He'd fought rebels, but he hadn't seen the civil wars, or the things that had been necessary in their wake. Rupert probably thought that he was a man without limits, but the Dowager had found out the hard way that she would do *whatever* was necessary to secure the throne for her family.

Still, it wasn't worth thinking about. This would be over soon. Sebastian would be safely back with his family, Rupert would have avenged his humiliation, and two girls who should have been long dead would go to the grave without a trace.

CHAPTER SIX

"It's a test," Kate whispered to herself as she stalked her victim. "It's a test."

She kept saying it to herself, perhaps in the hope that repetition would make it true, perhaps because it was the only way to keep herself following after Gertrude Illiard, keeping to the shadows while she sat on the balcony of her home for breakfast, slipping silently through the crowds of the city while the merchant's daughter walked with friends through the early morning markets.

Savis Illiard kept dogs and guards to protect his property and his daughter both, but the guards had been at their posts too long and relied on the dogs, while the dogs were easy to quiet with a flicker of power.

Kate watched the woman she was supposed to kill, and the truth was that she could have done it a dozen times over by now. She could have run up in the crowd and slid a knife between her ribs. She could have fired a crossbow bolt or even thrown a stone with lethal force. She could even have taken advantage of the environment of the city, startling a horse at the wrong moment or cutting the rope that held a barrel as her target walked beneath.

Kate did none of those things. She watched Gertrude Illiard instead.

It would have been easier if she had been an obviously evil person. If she had struck out at her father's servants in pique, or treated the people of the city like scum, Kate might have been able to see her as just a step away from the nuns who had tormented her, or the people who had looked down on her on the street. Instead, she was kind, in the small ways that people could be when they didn't think too much about it. She gave money to a beggar boy as she passed. She asked after the children of a shopkeeper she barely knew.

She seemed like a kind, gentle person, and Kate couldn't believe that even Siobhan would want someone like that dead.

"It's a test," Kate told herself again. "It has to be."

She tried to tell herself that the kindness had to be a façade masking some deeper, darker side. Perhaps this young woman

30

showed a kind face to the world to hide murders or blackmail, cruelty or deception. Yet while someone else might be able to tell themselves that, Kate could see Gertrude Illiard's thoughts, and none of them pointed to a predator lurking beneath the surface. She was a normal enough young woman for her place in the world, made wealthy by her father's business, perhaps a little unconcerned about it, but genuinely innocent in every respect Kate could see.

It was hard not to feel disgusted at what Siobhan commanded her to do then, and at what Kate had become under her tutelage. How could Siobhan want her dead? How could she demand that Kate do this thing? Was she really asking it just to see if Kate had it in her to kill on command? Kate hated that thought. She couldn't, she wouldn't, do such a thing.

But she had no choice, and she hated that even more.

She had to be sure, though, so she slipped back to the merchant's house ahead of her prey, slipping over the wall in a moment when she could feel that the guards weren't watching and sprinting to the shadows of the wall. She waited another few heartbeats, making sure that everything was still, then clambered up to the balcony to Gertrude Illiard's room. There was a latch on the balcony, but that was an easy thing to lift using a slender knife, letting her pad inside.

The room was empty, and Kate couldn't sense anyone nearby, so she quickly searched it. She didn't know what she was hoping to find. A vial of poison saved for a rival, perhaps. A diary detailing all the tortures she planned to inflict on someone. There was a diary, but even at a glance, Kate could see that it simply detailed the other young woman's dreams and hopes for the future, her meetings with friends, her brief flash of feelings for a young player she'd met in the market.

The truth was that Kate couldn't find a single reason why Gertrude Illiard deserved to die, and even though she'd killed before, Kate found the thought of murdering someone for no reason abhorrent. It made her sick just to think about doing it.

She felt the flicker of an approaching mind and swiftly hid under the bed, trying to think, trying to decide what she would do. It wasn't that this young woman reminded Kate of herself, because Kate couldn't imagine this merchant's daughter ever truly knowing suffering, or wanting to pick up a blade. She wasn't even like Sophia, because Kate's sister had a deceptive streak when she needed it, and the kind of hard practicality that came from having to live with nothing. This girl would never have spent weeks pretending to be something she wasn't, and would never have seduced a prince.

While a servant went around the room, tidying it in preparation for her mistress's return, Kate put her hand to the locket at her neck, thinking of the picture of a woman inside. Maybe that was it. Maybe Gertrude Illiard fit with the picture of well-born innocence Kate had when it came to her parents. What did that mean, though? Did it mean that she couldn't kill her? She touched the ring that sat beside the locket, intended for Sophia. She knew what her sister would say, but this wasn't a choice that Sophia would ever be in a position to have to make.

Then Gertrude came into the room, and Kate knew that she would have to make her choice soon. Siobhan was waiting, and Kate doubted that her teacher's patience would last forever.

"Thank you, Milly," Gertrude said. "Is my father home?"

"He isn't expected back for a couple of hours, miss."

"In that case, I think I will take a nap. I woke too early today."

"Of course, miss. I'll see that you aren't disturbed."

The servant walked off, shutting the door to the room behind her with a click. Kate saw embroidered boots pulled off and set down next to her hiding place, felt the shifting of the bed above her as Gertrude Illiard sat down on it. The timbers creaked as she lay down, and still Kate waited.

She had to do this. She'd seen what would happen to her if she didn't. Siobhan had made it clear: Kate was hers now, to do with as she wished. Kate was as tightly bound to her as she would have been if her debt had been sold to another. More tightly, because now it wasn't just the law of the land giving Siobhan power over Kate, but the magic of her fountain.

If she failed Siobhan in this, at best, she would find herself sent off into some living hell, forced to endure things that would make the House of the Unclaimed look like a palace. At worst... Kate had seen the ghosts of those who had betrayed Siobhan. She had seen what they suffered. Kate wouldn't join them, whatever it took.

She just had to keep reminding herself that this was a test.

She watched Gertrude's thoughts as she fell asleep, noting their changing rhythms as she slid into slumber. There was silence around the room now, as servants kept away to let their mistress get her rest. It was the perfect moment. Kate knew she had to act now, or not at all.

She slid out from under the bed without making a sound, rising back to her feet and looking down at Gertrude Illiard. In sleep, she

32

looked even more innocent, mouth slightly open as she lay with her head on one of a pair of goose down pillows.

It's a test, Kate told herself, *only a test. Siobhan will stop this before I kill her.*

It was the only thing that made sense. The woman of the fountain had no reason to want this girl dead, and Kate wouldn't believe that even she could be that capricious. Yet how did she pass the test? The only way that she could see was to actually try to murder this girl.

Kate stood there contemplating her options. She didn't have any poisons, and wouldn't know the best way to administer them if she did, so that was out. There was no way to engineer an accident here, the way she might have on the street. She could take out a dagger and cut Gertrude's throat, but would that leave enough of an opportunity for Siobhan to intervene? What if she stabbed or cut so fast that there was no saving the target of this test?

There was one obvious answer, and Kate contemplated it, lifting one of the silken pillows. It had a river scene from some far-off land woven into it, the raised threads rough under her fingers. She held it between her hands, stepping so that she stood over Gertrude Illiard, the pillow poised.

Kate felt the shift in the young woman's thoughts as she heard something, and saw her eyes snap open.

"What... what is this?" she asked.

"I'm sorry," Kate said, and bore down with the pillow.

Gertrude fought, but she wasn't strong enough to dislodge Kate. With the strength the fountain had unlocked, Kate could hold the pillow in place easily. She could feel the young woman struggling to find any space in which to breathe, or scream, or fight, but Kate kept her weight down over the pillow, not allowing the least crack of air to sneak through.

She wanted to reassure Gertrude that it would be all right; tell her that in a minute, Siobhan would stop this. She wanted to tell her that as bad as it felt now, it would all be fine. She couldn't, though. If she said it, there was too much of a risk that Siobhan would know that she wasn't treating this as real, and force her to go through with it. There was too much of a risk that Siobhan would throw her soul into the hellish depths of the fountain.

She had to be strong. She had to keep going.

Kate kept the pillow in place while Gertrude thrashed and clawed at her. She kept it in place even when her struggles started to weaken. When she went still, Kate looked around, half expecting

Siobhan to appear from nowhere to congratulate her, revive Gertrude Illiard, and declare this done.

Instead, there was only silence.

Kate pulled the pillow away from the young woman's face, and astonishingly, she still looked peaceful, despite the violence of the seconds before that moment. There was no life there in that expression, none of the animation that there had been while Kate had been following her around the city.

She could feel that there were no thoughts there to sense, but even so, she put her fingers to the pulse at Gertrude Illiard's throat. There was nothing. The young woman was gone, and Kate…

"I killed her," Kate said. She stuffed the pillow back into place beneath the merchant's daughter, beneath her *victim*, and stumbled back from the bed as if she'd been shoved. Her feet caught the boots that Gertrude had kicked off, and Kate fell, scrambling back to her feet in a hurry. "I killed her."

She hadn't believed that it would happen, not really. She hated herself in that moment. She'd killed before, but never like this. Never someone so helpless, so innocent.

"Miss, is everything all right?" the servant's voice called from the other side of the door.

Kate wanted to stand there, to let the ground swallow her up, to let people find her and kill her for what she'd done. She deserved it, and more than that. The full horror of what she'd just done started to dawn on her. She'd stood over an innocent woman and smothered her to death, with nothing quick or clean or gentle about it.

She deserved death for that. She should just stand there and let the merchant's guards give her it. She didn't, though. Woodenly, stumbling, Kate made her way back to the balcony. Around her, she could sense the guards springing into life as they started to understand that something was wrong.

A few more seconds, and there would be no way to escape. The guards would be hunting for intruders, and then Kate would have to fight to get clear. She would have to kill again, too, because if anyone recognized her later, she wouldn't be able to go back to the forge, or to Lord Cranston's company.

That thought was enough to drive her forward, sending her into a leap from the balcony that ended in a roll across the hard ground. Kate was up and running then, sprinting for the outer wall even as she pushed the dogs away from her with a burst of fear. She planted her feet on the wall, running up it and then leaping to catch the top. Kate hauled herself over, the way she might have pulled herself into a tree back in the forest. She leapt again, landing lightly on the other side and quickly losing herself in the crowds of the city's streets.

As she did it, Kate couldn't work out who she hated more, Siobhan or herself. Maybe she didn't need to choose. Maybe, after what she'd just done, there was enough hatred to be found for both of them. Kate knew one thing—she was going to find Siobhan, and she was going to get answers.

CHAPTER SEVEN

Sophia was running around the halls of a great house, and there was joy there, not flames. She and Kate were laughing, her sister's smaller hands reaching up for the bronze figurine of a horse, the edge of a tablecloth.

"Be careful, girls," Anora called from behind them, the nanny following along in their wake. "You mustn't disturb your father."

But I want Daddy, Kate sent over to Sophia. *I want to play soldiers.*

We could find Mother, Sophia sent back. *She could tell us a story.*

Sophia loved listening to old stories told in that beautiful, peaceful-sounding voice: *Bren and the Giant, The Seven Sisters of the Island;* it seemed that their mother knew more stories than there were stars in the sky, telling them about all the old creatures of magic that were now so rare they barely touched the world.

They laughed again and ran on, a conversation only they could hear whispering between them. They ran and hid, playing hide and seek while men and women brought in barrels and boxes and chests and sacks. They didn't talk about the possibility of a siege, but Sophia knew anyway. She and Kate always knew.

In spite of Anora's words, she found Kate heading toward her father's study. Sophia followed, and now she could hear her father arguing with a man who looked too much like Sebastian for it to be a coincidence. She frowned, wondering who Sebastian was, and why it should matter.

"I told you, Henry, I have no interest in your throne, whatever your spies say."

"But you still side with the rebels."

"Agreeing that there should be some kind of assembly is not the same thing as fighting against you."

"It is *exactly* the same!"

Sophia wanted to stay and hear the rest, but she was standing in a hall of mirrors now, and it seemed that every mirror held a scene of her parents' lives. It was only as she saw it that she realized she was dreaming, not there in truth. She saw them first meeting, falling in love in a way that reminded her heartbreakingly of her and Sebastian. She saw them riding through their lands dispensing justice and helping people who had nothing.

There were darker scenes too. The civil wars came, in a swirl of blood and musket smoke. Sophia saw her father fighting in battle, heard her mother arguing with courtiers she didn't recognize.

"I don't care if we do have the blood, trying to claim the throne now would just cost more lives."

Sophia saw more battles, and tense scenes around a great house she knew from a thousand other dreams. There was no context for it, and the images shifted too fast for Sophia to follow more than a few glimpses of each. As with so many of her dreams, she had the feeling that this was more, but she didn't understand it, couldn't place all the details.

She drifted on to a fresh set of mirrors, and for a moment she thought that she was looking at herself. The deep red hair was the same, and so were the features, but there was something in the girl who stood there that reminded her of Sebastian as well. Somehow, Sophia knew that this was their daughter.

The image flickered, then vanished.

Sophia plunged deeper into the endless hall of mirrors, trying to see more of what might happen, trying to understand, but the mirrors seemed to open out onto every facet of the world, and it was hard to tell what was real and what was imaginary, what was happening now and what might still be to happen. There was too much of it. There was simply...

Sophia woke with a gasp in the morning light, because the pressure of all those futures had felt so real, so immediate. She blinked, trying to make sense of it all and judge if anything she'd seen was real. It felt real. Sophia could still see the face of her daughter, and she *wanted* that to be real.

She wanted it, but even so, she hesitated. This was such a dangerous world to bring a child into, and such a dangerous situation. She couldn't offer the safety of a grand house, or the peace of a settled life. She couldn't even offer her child a father, because Sebastian was out there somewhere, separated from her by distance and his family's pressures.

Even so, Sophia couldn't think about the face she'd seen without feeling a deep wave of love. She wanted to see her daughter, watch her grow up into that.

Of course, for that to happen, at least one thing had to happen first. Sophia took hold of the powder pouch Cora had given her, balancing it, staring at it. Then she stood and threw it, sending it as

37

far from her as she could manage, away onto the mossy ground in the distance.

***

It took even longer than it looked to reach the great house, because the hills and the trees of Monthys worked to stretch out the space around them, forcing the road to wind rather than proceeding in a straight line. There were moments when Sophia couldn't see the house at all, and it was only guesswork whether they were going in the right direction.

The roads were empty this morning, without the occasional travelers Sophia was used to passing. The whole space felt quiet, almost abandoned, or simply so remote that there *was* no one else to pass. Their cart rumbling along the road was the loudest thing around by far.

Sophia had to admit that the landscape around them was beautiful. Monthys had rolling hills lined with moss-covered boulders, trees of shimmering green and red, and brooks that ran alongside the path, bubbling and foaming as they hit stones. Sophia could imagine... no, she could *remember*, those hills covered in snow in the winter, when the whole place turned into a thing of stark, beautiful white and no one could travel on the roads.

Thankfully, there was no snow on the ground now, and the cart could still make its way along the road without any problems beyond the occasional windblown branch. Around them, birds twittered in the trees, and the wind blew through the gaps in the hills. Somewhere above, Sophia saw a buzzard circling, obviously on the hunt for the hares that crouched low among the moss. There were even a few sheep, with the wild look of things left to fend for themselves for most of the year.

Sophia started to see other animal signs, too, more worrying ones. There were scratches on some of the trees they passed, obviously some kind of territorial marking, and prints by the side of the road that indicated an animal bigger than anything they'd seen so far.

Somewhere in the distance, Sophia heard a howl, the sound of a wolf's voice bouncing off the sides of the hills around them. It was a high, piercing note that seemed to last longer than it should, sustained by its echoes as it claimed the space around it. There was no answering chorus from a pack, but maybe that just meant they were being quiet.

Sophia could feel the nervousness of the others at that sound. Cora started looking around as if expecting a pack of wolves to leap out at any moment. Emeline was still, but she had a look that said she was stretching out her own powers, trying to find any sense of approaching danger. As for Sienne, the forest cat started, and then ran off the path, into a patch of trees.

"Sienne, wait," Sophia called after her, reinforcing the instruction with a pulse of her mental abilities. The forest cat ignored it, quickly disappearing from sight. Was she scared, or hungry, or just being wary?

"She'll be all right," Emeline said. She looked around again. "It's us I'm worried about. Whatever made that sound is close. We need to keep moving."

They kept going, pushing the horses forward faster now. Before, it had been easy to appreciate the beauty of the surrounding countryside, but now Sophia found herself watching it for signs of the creature that had made the sound they'd heard. She reached out with her powers, trying to pick out the minds of approaching creatures the way she was able to touch Sienne's mind, but it was hard to differentiate between them, or to know if any of them posed a threat.

At least one of them did, though, because a little way further on, they found a body.

It took a moment to identify it as human, because large parts of it were missing. It lay at the side of the road, obviously pulled there by whatever had attacked it. The remains of rough-spun clothes hinted at a farmer or a herder, perhaps a shepherd to some of the sheep that Sophia had seen out on the hills. Whoever this person had been, they were long past any kind of help.

"We should bury them," Cora said. "We should give them that much dignity at least."

"There's no time," Emeline replied. "What if the thing that did this comes back?"

They looked over to Sophia, and it seemed that she was going to get to make the final decision. Before she could do so, however, she felt the flicker of a mind in the trees near the road.

A wolf padded out, and it was a long way from being one of the scrawny pack wolves that people sometimes hunted to keep their animals safe. This thing was at least as high as Sophia's waist at the shoulder, with dark fur and a ruff at its throat almost like a lion's mane. Its eyes had a golden shine to them, and its teeth, when it bared them, seemed like daggers.

It growled as it approached.

"Send it away," Emeline said to Sophia. "If you manage to control that cat of yours, maybe you can manage it with this wolf."

Sophia wanted to point out that Emeline had her own powers, but this wasn't the time. Instead, she reached out, touching the mind of the advancing wolf, trying to soothe it. She found only madness and violence. This wasn't an animal that could be soothed or persuaded. It was a thing without a pack, driven to kill by an anger that nothing could control.

Even as Sophia thought that, it leapt. The horses reared, and one screamed as the lone wolf's teeth fastened onto its throat. Blood splashed, and Sophia felt the head of it against her skin.

"Get up into the trees," she yelled to the others.

They didn't need to be told twice. Emeline ran from the cart to the nearest tree, with Cora following in her wake. Sophia had a moment of staring at the wolf as it brought down one of their cart horses, then she slashed through the reins that held the other with a knife, at least giving it a chance at survival.

She sprinted for the tree, and as she ran, she heard the wolf bark, rushing in behind her. She ran to the trunk and leapt, grabbing for the branches even as she felt teeth pulling at the hem of her dress. She heard it tear and didn't care, just struggling to get up out of the beast's way. Emeline and Cora caught her arms, pulling her up onto the thick branches near the heart of the tree.

"Wolves can't climb, can they?" Cora asked.

"They can't climb," Emeline said. "But they can be patient."

Sure enough, the lone wolf was down on the ground, staring up at them. Would it go away, given time? Sophia had to hope so. She tried to push it away with her talent, but its mind was still a closed thing of hunger and violence.

"There's something wrong with it," she said. "It feels like there's no way into its mind."

"It might be rabid," Emeline guessed. "Or it might just be something so violent that even you can't affect it. Probably it was forced out of its pack for a reason."

Whatever it was, Sophia couldn't affect the creature, which meant that they were stuck. They could sit there until the wolf got bored, but if that didn't happen, then they would stay there until they slept or starved, or just got too weak to cling onto the tree. Then it would have them.

Then Sophia saw a familiar flicker of soft gray fur, and her heart tightened.

Sienne, don't!

It was too late though, because the young forest cat was already flinging herself forward. She was smaller than the wolf, and younger, and certainly less insane, but the forest cat still slammed into it in a flurry of fur that knocked the wolf to the ground.

The next few seconds were impossible to follow, as the two animals struck and wrestled, growled and fought. The wolf tried to bring its teeth to bear, but Sienne struck out with both teeth and claws, twisting impossibly as she raked the wolf with them. In an instant, she was behind it, and her teeth clamped down on the wolf's neck.

Sophia heard a crack, and the wolf went limp.

She rushed down from the tree, hurrying to Sienne. The forest cat had blood on her coat, but it was impossible to see if any of it was her own. Sophia hugged her close, not caring if she got blood on her dress.

"That was such a dangerous thing to do," Sophia whispered. "You could have been killed."

But the cat hadn't been. Instead, she'd slain the wolf, and now she purred, licking Sophia's hand as Sophia made sure the cat wasn't wounded. She wasn't. More than that, she'd saved them. Sophia held onto her, looking around. One of their horses was dead, while the other had run and was nowhere to be seen. Their cart was too heavy to move by hand, and anyway, there were only so many supplies left on it. She looked ahead to where the estate still sat, beckoning her onward, then turned back to the others.

"It looks as though we have to walk from here."

CHAPTER EIGHT

By the time Sebastian reached the town of Barriston, both he and his horse were exhausted. He felt as though he might fall from it with every stride the creature took, while his horse was lathered in sweat, ridden far too hard for far too long. Sebastian had changed mounts a half dozen times at coaching inns along the way, but even so, he knew that he had pushed this one close to its limits.

He'd hoped that he might overtake Sophia on the way, but it seemed that with her head start, even the narrow width of his mother's domain was too much to cover before she made it to the town.

Barriston. Sebastian looked at it from the top of a rise leading down to it, and his first impression was of a large brown stain on the landscape. Unlike Ashton, which had long since spilled past its walls, Barriston had managed to keep adjusting itself to fit, even rebuilding them after the civil wars. Sebastian knew that had nothing to do with defending it, though. It was simply the easiest way to ensure that the town's burgomasters got the tolls for the roads in and out.

"Why would you come here, Sophia?" Sebastian asked the air, but there was no obvious reason. Maybe she'd thought that a town that produced half the things Ashton needed would be a good place to find work, or maybe she just wanted to lose herself. Maybe she had friends here, or maybe it had simply been a random choice.

Whatever the reason, Sebastian would find her.

He rode down, and there were watchmen on the town gates, armed with clubs and short swords, looking as though they were mostly there to look after the short man in a clerk's clothes who sat by a table there.

"State your name and your business in the city," the man said, barely looking up, "then prepare any bags for inspection for goods taxable under the town statutes."

The watchmen stared at Sebastian in a way that said that, even if they didn't know quite who he was, they still recognized someone of importance when they saw them. The clerk, meanwhile, barely glanced up from his ledger, his quill poised.

"Quickly now," he said. "I don't have all day."

"Prince Sebastian of the House of Flamberg," Sebastian said. "I'm here because there is someone I need to find, and as for the taxes, since they ought to be remitted to my mother's treasury, maybe we should ignore them for now."

He could see the shock on the other man's face as he looked up. Sebastian waited. He didn't like relying on his position like that, but he also didn't like men who tried to use their minor roles to bully others.

"So, may I enter the town?" he asked.

"Of course, your highness," the man said. "I am sure that the burgomaster will be honored to see you."

Sebastian didn't particularly care about that. He just wanted to dive into the city and find Sophia. Of course, the problem with *that* was that there were too many people to sort through them all, even if Barriston was smaller than Ashton. Maybe accepting the burgomaster's hospitality would help.

Which was why he found himself given an escort through the streets and led to a town hall that looked as though it had only just been finished in gleaming marble. There were statues outside, and unlike Ashton, these weren't the usual blank-faced accolades to the Masked Goddess, but instead seemed to be of merchants who had, the inscriptions said, rebuilt the city after the wars. Sebastian wondered if any of the builders or stonemasons or carpenters actually doing the work had statues.

He found himself led inside, through a series of offices where priests and clerks worked at ledgers without looking up, to an office where he found himself greeted by a middle-aged man in rich purple and red.

"Your highness, welcome to Barriston. I am Sir Julian Moreston, burgomaster of the city. We were not expecting your visit. Is this an official matter on behalf of your mother?"

"A matter of importance to me," Sebastian said. "There is a young woman I am trying to locate."

He saw the burgomaster frown. "And does Ashton not have many young women?"

It seemed clear that the other man didn't want him there. Who could blame him? Probably he suspected that a visit from Sebastian would be like one from Rupert: a dangerous disruption, and a threat to anyone who contradicted him.

"I was told that this particular one would be coming in this direction," Sebastian said. "A red-haired young woman called Sophia, and possibly using the name Sophia of Meinhalt, traveling

43

on a cart with two others. She would have arrived in Barriston recently, probably within the last few days."

"Many people enter the city," Sir Julian pointed out.

"And you keep records of all of them," Sebastian said.

The burgomaster shrugged at that, gesturing to the piles of paperwork that had made it to his desk.

"I keep records of everything. The trick is finding what is needed. Is this girl rich enough that she would buy a house here to stay in?"

Sebastian shook his head. "As far as I know, she has very little money with her."

"Is she connected enough to the right people that she would be invited to the parties my wife insists on throwing?" Sir Julian asked, with the air of a man who had sat through too many of them.

Again, Sebastian shook his head, although this was less certain. "She *might* try to find a way in though."

He heard Sir Julian sigh. "I really don't have enough time, your highness."

And Sebastian couldn't afford to spend another moment away from Sophia if it could be prevented. "I know you must be a busy man, but please, will you at least ask the men who keep records at the gates if they have seen her?"

"You think they would remember her?" Sir Julian replied.

Sebastian couldn't imagine anyone seeing Sophia and forgetting her. Just the sight of her was like the sun coming out from behind a cloud.

"Yes, they would remember her."

"Oh, so she's beautiful," Sir Julian said. He went over to a window, pointing out to the city. "I'll ask, but if a beautiful girl with no money or connections comes to the city, there's really only one part of it she'll end up in. Go to the theater district. If she's here, she'll be there. Just... be prepared for how you might find her."

***

As soon as Sebastian started to wander through the theater district, he began to understand Sir Julian's warning. The district probably didn't deserve its name, as there was only one real playhouse that Sebastian could see, standing in the middle of the district with its gaudily painted walls and its signs proclaiming the latest performances of Granston's *The Seventh King*.

44

Around it, though, there was plenty of entertainment of a more dubious character. The coffee houses looked as likely to sell dream resin or golden-smoke as the imports of the Near Colonies. There were warehouses that looked as though they'd been converted to fighting pits for men, dogs, or other animals. There were smaller supposed theaters, but one look at them told Sebastian that the "performances" they put on had little to do with high art. Then there were the brothels, which seemed to have sprung up on every corner like mushrooms, declaring that they catered to every possible taste.

Not Sebastian's. There was only one woman he was interested in finding in this mess.

He searched through it anyway, looking out for anyone who might be Sophia, or who might have a clue where she was. It was hard to imagine her coming here, yet where else would she be able to go, given that she was running away? Where was better to hide than somewhere like this?

Sebastian trawled through it all, doing his best to ignore what he saw even as his eyes skimmed over the writhing bodies and semi-conscious, drug-addled souls to try to catch any glimpse of Sophia.

In a coffee house reeking of cheap perfume and sweat from the bawdy houses on either side, Sebastian thought he caught a glimpse of flame red hair. It was enough to catch his attention, and as he stopped he heard the argument.

"You stupid bitch!" a man roared. He had the bulk and the muscles of a porter or a warehouseman, a shaven head and bare lower arms worked with tattoos that had little beauty to them. He stood over a woman, and all Sebastian could see of her was that flash of long red hair. "You don't get to say no to me!"

He pulled a hand back, and Sebastian heard the slap ringing around the room. He ran forward on instinct, slamming into the larger man, hitting him below the knees and sending them both crashing down into a table. Cups fell and shattered, while somewhere further away a woman screamed.

"No one treats Sophia like that," Sebastian said, coming up on top as the two fought for position. The big man tried to shove him off with all the strength of those huge muscles, but Sebastian was the one who'd been forced to train for battle, and he rode the movement, staying in place as he struck downward with closed fists. He felt his skin crack and scrape as his fists slammed into the other man's shaven skull, but Sebastian didn't care. All that mattered was that this man had just struck the woman he—

He looked up and saw that it wasn't Sophia. The woman there was older than her, and thinner, made to look almost skeletally so by whatever drugs she'd spent her life consuming there. It was only as Sebastian looked that he realized that she was the one who was screaming.

In that moment of distraction, the big man shoved him off, coming up on top with his own fists raised. Sebastian managed to dodge the first blow, then took the second on his arms.

"Damn nobles," the man roared. "Coming in here, thinking they can take what isn't theirs!"

Sebastian managed to get his legs in between them, then kicked up, catching the other man on the jaw. He rolled to his feet as the thug struggled upward, and the big man reached into his tunic, the hand coming out with a knife.

With no time to draw his sword, Sebastian blocked the first thrust, punching him hard. He managed to get both hands onto the knife arm, striking with his head, his knees, his feet. He shoved the other man back, sending him sprawling as he wrenched the knife away.

Then something hit him on the back of the head hard enough that he saw stars. Sebastian spun, and the movement only made him stagger. He saw the red-haired woman holding the remains of a bottle, the rest of which had scattered around him as she broke it over his head.

He collapsed to his knees, and the thug with the knife was already retrieving it.

"That, I think, is quite enough." Sebastian recognized Sir Julian's voice instantly. He spun and found the city's burgomaster standing there, accompanied by a couple of burly watchmen. "If the man with the knife moves, deal with it. Your highness, if you would care to accompany me?"

There was enough sharpness to the way he said it to make it clear that it wasn't a request, whatever their difference in rank. It took Sebastian two attempts to get to his feet, but he went along with it because he still needed this man's help, walking out while the watchmen kept their hands on their clubs and their eyes on the man Sebastian had been fighting.

Out on the street, Sebastian threw up. The blow to his head was still making the world swim. As he came back to himself, he saw a carriage. He also saw the change in Sir Julian's expression.

"Get in," the burgomaster said.

"I'm still a prince," Sebastian pointed out.

"A prince who has been going around my city visiting every whorehouse and fighting with its citizens," Sir Julian snapped back. "I had heard that was your brother's manner of behaving, but now I see that it is his entire family. Get in. I will drive you to the gates."

Sebastian got into the carriage, sitting opposite the other man and trying to remain calm.

"I have been searching through the worst of the city because you pointed me in that direction," Sebastian said. He wasn't going to be rebuked when he'd done nothing wrong. "I fought with that man because he was in the middle of attacking a woman. Maybe this is a city where you allow such things, but I will not."

"What we allow or disallow is a matter for the law," Sir Julian said, "not a prince who thinks he can do as he pleases."

It made Sebastian wonder which side Sir Julian had been on in the last of the civil wars. The powers of the monarchy had been restricted for a reason.

"I'm not trying to cause trouble," Sebastian said. "I'm just trying to find someone I love."

"Well, you won't find her in Barriston," Sir Julian said. "That is why I came to find you. I did as you asked, and sought out the clerks who have worked on the gates in the past two weeks. None of them saw a cart with three women, one of them with red hair. None of them has heard of this 'Sophia' of yours. She is not in the city."

He said it bluntly, as if there were no other way that she could have gotten into Barriston. Sebastian suspected that it wasn't as simple as that. There might be another way in, without being seen, but then, how would Sophia know it? Why would she bother, when this was a city where no one knew her?

No, Sir Julian was right. Sophia wasn't there.

That thought hit Sebastian as hard as the musket ball that had struck him fighting on the Strait Islands. He didn't want to believe it, but it was the truth, wasn't it? He'd traveled so much faster than any cart could have, but there had been no sign of Sophia on the road. He'd asked around the city, and there was no word. Now its burgomaster told him that there was no record of her. The last time he'd heard anything of Sophia had been at the crossroads, when…

…when he'd allowed himself to be tricked.

Sophia hadn't gone west at all, had she? She must have gone north, and then either she'd told the man there to fool him, or he'd decided to do it out of some drunken sense of malice. If Sophia didn't want to be found, what did that mean? Was she in danger? Did she not love him?

Both of those thoughts felt like knives to the heart. Sebastian sat there, wondering, while Sir Julian's carriage conveyed him to the gate.

"I'll need a fresh horse when I get there," Sebastian said.

"A *fresh* horse?" Sir Julian asked.

"I'll have to ride hard."

As hard as he had coming here, because he wasn't going to stop. He was going to ride back to the crossroads, and then ride north. He was going to ride as far as he needed to. He would do whatever it took.

He had to find Sophia.

CHAPTER NINE

Angelica found that she quite enjoyed the freedom that came with riding alone. There was no need to ride in a rickety carriage to accommodate maids and ladies-in-waiting too delicate to mount a horse. There was no need to ride side-saddle, as propriety might have demanded had she been following along after a hunt. Even her riding clothes were a distinct improvement on the usual confinements of corsetry and tightly laced dresses.

Then there was the prospect of being rid of Sophia at the end of this. That was a pleasurable thought in itself.

Of course, there were downsides to the journey. Angelica didn't like being away from Ashton for so long, because she had no doubt that the other women of the royal court would plot and scheme while she was away. Briefly, Angelica found herself thinking of some of the women whose reputations she had destroyed: the marchioness who had found herself the subject of unceasing rumors about what she did with her serving girls, the daughter of an earl who had found her unguarded comments about Rupert's behavior relayed back to him.

It wouldn't have to be much: a word in the right ears suggesting that her absence involved running off with some man, perhaps, or some time spent prying her friends loose from the circle Angelica had so carefully built. Not all plots involved a knife, although Angelica certainly had no problems with those that did.

No, the less time she spent away from the city, the better.

Besides, what did the country beyond it actually *have* that was so good? Angelica spent as little time as possible on her parents' country estate, and tried to confine it to those portions of the year when there were likely to be festivals and dances in a long, slow circuit of all the houses in the Shires. That at least offered opportunities for entertainment in the spaces away from the city where there were fewer eyes on her.

Without that, the countryside mostly seemed to be an endless expanse of trees and blank, boring fields. Angelica knew that such things were necessary to produce food, but did there really have to be so many of them? It seemed like a waste of space that could be used for more *civilized* things. Even an inn or two that didn't look as though it was about to fall down would be an improvement on what Angelica had found so far.

She kept riding, her horse seemingly tireless as she made her way through streams and over hills, along roads and down through forested sections. That was only to be expected: the beast was, after all, of the finest stock that her father had been able to bring in from the continent's stables. Blood mattered in these things, as in so much else.

Perhaps if Sebastian could be brought to realize that, then he would cease this nonsense of trying to find Sophia. Then again, Angelica knew what men could be like. Probably he would continue to follow after her like a lovesick puppy for as long as she was out there somewhere. Angelica would need to deal with that if she was ever going to convince him that their bloodlines were too well suited to ignore the possibility of a match.

When she came to a fast-flowing river, Angelica found signs of what had probably once been a ferry crossing. The rope to pull it across was long since gone, though. It meant that she had to ride parallel to the river for close to an hour before she found a patch of water shallow enough to ride through. Had Sophia had to do this? Had she had to ride her stolen cart back up along the riverbank until she could find the road again?

From time to time on the road, Angelica passed people. Mostly they looked like common folk, walking from field to home and back again. Some of them looked like tinkers or traveling merchants. Angelica stopped everyone, wanting to make sure that she was still on the right path.

After all, she knew exactly how easy it was to send someone on the wrong route.

"You there," she called down to a man in rough clothes. "Have you seen three women on a cart, one of them with red hair?"

"Aye," the man said, as if that were an appropriate way for him to talk to his betters. "I saw them. They came to the inn. The Braen brothers were there, and the eldest... well, she set a beast on him the likes of which I wouldn't have believed if I hadn't seen it."

"Set a beast on him?" Angelica said.

"Like a great cat it was," the man replied, "but it was like a thing possessed!"

Angelica laughed at that. "With fire in its eyes and smoke curling from its fur?"

The yokel stared up at her. "You might not believe it, but I saw what I saw."

50

Half of it deep drowned in beer, no doubt. Angelica could no more believe that Sophia had summoned some kind of demon cat than that she could fly. To avoid having to listen to any more of that drivel, she rode on.

There was a village some way ahead. Sophia rode toward it and stopped at its inn, handing her reins off to a stable boy with the kind of smile that would probably have him stumbling about his work with thoughts of her.

She went inside, and one look at the place told her that the food would be a thousand miles from quail or venison, or spun sugar or fine wine. Even so, she ordered stew, sitting by herself and sipping watered beer that tasted as though the barrel had been open for a month. When she couldn't stand it anymore, she held up a coin for the room to see.

"Do any of you peasants have information on a woman with red hair named Sophia?" she asked. "Do you know where she was going?"

"A woman like that passed through," one man called. "She headed off in the direction of the old bridge and the estates in Monthys."

Angelica tossed the coin vaguely in his direction, letting the men scrabble over it as she left and snatching the reins to her mare from the boy who was scrubbing her down. She didn't want to stay in a flea-infested wreck of a village like this one moment longer than she had to.

Instead, Angelica rode on along tree-lined roads and between hills with almost sheer sides. It was colder here than it had been in the south of the country, but she would worry about that once she had found Sophia. Maybe she could make a bonfire out of her cart, or a cloak from this demon cat she was supposed to have.

Angelica was still thinking of that with amusement when two figures stepped out of the rocks ahead of her. It was obvious from the start what their intentions were; innocent people didn't hide like that, or wear half masks and broad hats to disguise themselves. One was a man, one a woman, although they were both dressed in shirt and breeches, with long jackets and scarves. The richness of their clothes suggested that they could have belonged to nobles, although it was also fairly obvious that if they had, they had been stolen. A band of plaid in the colors of one of the clans suggested that these were thieves down from the mountains to the far north.

Highway robbers were things out of stories, to Angelica. Typically, she traveled with enough companions and bodyguards that anyone foolish enough to attack them would quickly find themselves hanging in a gibbet as a warning to others. Alone, though, things might be more difficult.

She tensed to kick her horse into a gallop, and the woman raised a pistol.

"I wouldn't," she said, her accent thick with the burrs to be found across the border. "'Twould be a shame to put a hole in such pretty riding clothes."

Angelica drew to a halt, considering her options. In the stories, highway robbers were always dashing and courteous, eloquent and fair to those who didn't try to trick them.

"Get down," the man said, in a clipped voice that had no hint of courtesy. He had a pistol of his own now. If Angelica tried to run, she had little doubt that she would die.

"There's really no need for violence," she said. "I'll cooperate."

"Oh, do you hear that?" the woman said, with a sneer in her tone. "She'll cooperate. As if she gets a choice."

"Maybe she's expecting us to kiss her hand and thank her for the privilege of robbing her," the man said with a laugh. "Well, thank you kindly, milady. Now give us all your gold or we'll put a lead ball between your eyes and take it anyway."

Angelica could feel the fear rising in her, but pushed it down as her hands went to her belt.

"Quickly, quickly!" the woman snapped, holding out a hand.

Angelica continued to fumble at her money pouch, and at one of the vials nearest it. Finally, it came loose. Angelica threw the pouch over with one gloved hand to land at the woman's feet.

"You'll pick it up and hand it to me properly," the woman snapped. "You think I'm a servant to scrabble around for your coins? Kneel and give me it."

"As you say," Angelica said. She didn't have to act to let fear seep into her voice. She knelt, picking up the bag and simultaneously dropping a small stream of clear liquid onto it from the vial that she'd palmed. She held it up. "Please, just don't hurt me."

"Just don't hurt me," the woman said in an imitation that amused no one but herself. She snatched the bag from Angelica's hands, taking it in one fleshy palm. "Haven't you worked out yet that you don't get to decide?"

"We can do what we want," the man agreed. His hand settled on Angelica's shoulder. "Maybe we'll take this pretty riding dress and the horse, leave you to stagger back to a village in an under-shift."

"Maybe we'll take you," the woman said, "and sell you for what you're worth."

Shock flooded through Angelica at that prospect. "I'm not one of the Indentured. No one would take me without their mark!"

The man laughed at that. "Oh, she's had a sheltered life if she thinks that a mark can't be applied to a calf. *Shall* we take her?"

The woman shook her head. "It's too far back. You want her, have her, maybe I'll take a turn too, but we cut her throat after."

"Please," Angelica begged. "I've given you what you wanted. There's no reason for this."

"Except that we want to," the man said. He pulled away his mask. The features underneath were flat and ugly, a long way from any image of a dashing robber that had ever been painted. "Up."

He hauled Angelica to her feet, pushing her back in the direction of a flat rock covered in moss.

"Please," Angelica tried again, but the man's hand tangled in her hair. "I'll do anything you want, just let me live."

"How about we see what you do, and then decide?" the man shot back. "What do you reckon, Elsie? Elsie?"

He was obviously waiting for an answer from his partner in crime, but the woman wasn't answering. Instead, her hands were clawing at her throat, gasps starting to come from her as she staggered amidst the moss.

"What's happening?" the man said. "Elsie, talk to me."

"She can't," Angelica said, her hand going to the folds of her dress. "Poison can make that kind of thing difficult."

"Poison?" the robber echoed. He turned back to her, and now the amusement was gone from his features. Now there was just anger. "You poisoned her?"

"Yes," Angelica said with a smile. "I don't know why that is such a hard concept to understand."

"You—"

They were already close, so Angelica didn't have to move forward much. Her hand just had to rise, bringing with it the wickedly sharp stiletto it now held. The blade was perhaps six inches long, but less than the width of a finger. Angelica thrust it up like a needle under the robber's ribcage, hearing him gasp as the blade went in.

"The heart can be difficult to find sometimes," she whispered, holding him almost as close as a lover. Behind them, his real lover was falling to the grass, twitching as the poison started to claim her. "There's a young man… his heart is proving to be very difficult indeed."

53

The robber didn't respond, because he was too busy gasping in pain.

"Then again, it's not a knife I'm trying to use with his," Angelica said. "Your heart seems to have been easy enough with one."

She stepped back before she pulled the stiletto out, because she didn't want to get blood on her riding gear. She pulled it clear and the blood spurted, and then the robber toppled forward. Angelica considered the two of them for a moment and then went over for her coin pouch, very carefully washing it clean using the thieves' water bottles.

On impulse, she set about robbing her attackers more thoroughly, taking their pistols, then one of the masks that they'd used, and a hat. She even took the clan plaid from the woman, because it occurred to her that there might be a situation where it would come in useful as a way of blaming the barbarous thugs.

She could, for example, leave it beside Sophia's body when she killed her.

CHAPTER TEN

Kate ran to Siobhan's wood with all the speed of her fury behind her. She plunged between the trees, shoving branches out of the way as she hurried toward the spot where the fountain stood. She half expected the wood to try to push her out, to try to shrink from her anger, but instead she found it almost drawing her forward so that she found the standing stones, the crumbling stairs, and finally the overgrown space where the fountain stood.

"Why so angry, Kate dear?" Siobhan asked. She stepped from the trees on the far side of the fountain. "Was my task not to your liking?"

Kate's hand closed on her sword. If she plunged it into the witch, would it kill her? Would it feel any better than it had when she'd just murdered a young woman? Siobhan was a long way from innocent.

"You know it wasn't," Kate said. "You just had me murder someone!"

"I told you that it was what I wanted before you set out," Siobhan said. She moved closer, sitting on the edge of the fountain, and it shimmered, moving from its crumbling present to the glory of the past in a moment.

"I didn't think you meant it!" Kate shouted back. "I thought it was a test."

Siobhan shrugged. "I am not responsible for what you think, apprentice. And it was a test. A test of whether you could bring yourself to kill on command. I even explained that test for you. And you passed. Well done."

"Well done?" Kate snarled. "Well *done?*"

She rushed forward, grabbing for Siobhan, her hands fastening in the silk of the other woman's dress.

"Consider carefully what you are about to do, Kate," Siobhan said. "I always do."

"I don't care what you do," Kate snapped back, but she still pushed Siobhan away from her. The woman of the fountain stood tall in the middle of it, and now the plants around the edge of the clearing rustled as they moved. Kate could see brambles rising up like whips. One, just one, lashed out, gouging a line of blood down Kate's arm. Kate forced herself not to react. She wouldn't give Siobhan the satisfaction of it.

"Don't you?" Siobhan said. "I could choose to flay the skin from your body. I could break your mind and leave you an empty thing at my feet. Are you sure you don't care what I choose to do?"

Would those brambles really be enough to stop Kate if she leapt at Siobhan? Somehow, Kate doubted it, but even so, she couldn't bring herself to try.

"She was *innocent*, Siobhan," Kate said. "I followed her. I read her thoughts. There wasn't an ounce of cruelty in her, and you still had me kill her. I smothered her because I thought you would tell me to stop. I didn't even give her a clean death."

"Perhaps you should have taken me at my word about wanting her dead," Siobhan said. "These things have their consequences, if not for you, then for others."

She said it as if the perfect solution would have been for Kate to simply stab Gertrude Illiard the first time she saw her, without asking questions, without agonizing over it, without so much as questioning the necessity of becoming a murderer.

"Do you even understand what this means to me?" Kate asked. "Do you understand how much it hurts?"

"Rather less than some of the alternatives, I imagine," Siobhan said. Her hand stirred the fountain's waters almost idly, and the reflections in it shifted to show the hellish place that housed the spirits of those who had betrayed her. Within it, Kate could hear the pitiful screams of the souls held there.

"Is that it?" Kate asked. "Is that your answer? More threats?"

The thought of that only fed her anger. She would kill Siobhan before she allowed her to send her to that place. She had kept her side of the bargain.

"Just a reminder that you are my apprentice," Siobhan said, "and you were required to perform the tasks I set."

That might have been good enough for some people. It had been the reason Kate had forced herself to go along with it, but it hadn't been the whole of it. She'd known that she had no choice, but no, that wasn't true. Siobhan had given her a choice. She *could* have chosen whatever vile fate the woman of the fountain had chosen for her instead. She could have been brave enough to suffer, and a young woman would have lived.

"At least tell me why," Kate said. "You wouldn't before, but tell me now."

"It was necessary," Siobhan said.

"That isn't an answer," Kate shot back. She thought about Gertrude as she'd been when Kate had followed her. She thought about the diary she'd found. "There was nothing evil about her, Siobhan. Why could you want her dead?"

Siobhan cocked her head to one side. "Yes, I suppose I owe you that now that you have shown that you will do what I command."

She hopped down from the fountain, waving her hand across it in a move that made it ripple as though some hidden current were working within it.

"What are you doing?" Kate asked.

"Watch," Siobhan said.

The waters shifted, and now they showed Gertrude Illiard's face, as it had been when Kate had been following her. It looked pristine, untouched by worry or by cruelty, not knowing the violence that would come to her soon at Kate's hands.

"She was innocent," Kate repeated.

"She was," Siobhan agreed. "For now. I told you before about the price of having power. Do you remember?"

Kate struggled to push her anger and impatience back long enough to remember.

"You said that if you know something is going to happen and you have the power to change it, then doing nothing is a choice."

"A choice with consequences," Siobhan said. She waved her hand over the fountain, and now it seemed that it shone with golden and silver strands. "Consequences I can see, if I focus."

"You can see the future," Kate said.

Siobhan smiled in a way that made it seem like a child's question.

"I can pick apart the chains of consequence," Siobhan said. "I can see some of what might be. Is it so hard for you to believe, apprentice, with all *you* have seen?"

Kate found herself thinking of the visions she'd seen. Of men in the uniforms of the New Army charging through the streets of Ashton. Of people dying while she tried to save them.

"Can things be changed?" Kate asked.

Siobhan nodded. "That is the question, isn't it? Yes, things can be changed, but every change has consequences, every touch on the balance setting the weight of lives into new configurations."

"And where does Gertrude Illiard fit into this?" Kate asked. "Are you telling me that you had me kill an innocent person just to change things in the future?"

Siobhan paused. "Perhaps I *should* have had you do that. Perhaps you needed to learn that lesson too: that one person is not worth the whole of a war. But no, that is not what I was doing here."

"Then what?" Kate demanded. She was getting sick of the way Siobhan was dancing around this. Her would-be teacher never seemed to be willing to give out a straight answer. She wanted Kate to be no more than a cog in her schemes, and Kate wasn't prepared to do that, whatever promises she'd made.

"You saw Gertrude Illiard as she was this morning," Siobhan said. "But I saw all the versions of her. I saw the girl who took on her father's business when he died of a heart attack a year from now. I saw the girl who found that he had debts and enemies. Who tried to do good, but found that the only way to maintain it all was to do worse and worse."

She waved a hand, and now there was another image of Gertrude in the water, looking older and less carefree. She was talking to someone Kate couldn't see.

"Tell the Far Colonies traders that we will agree to their terms," she said.

"But Madam Illiard, that will mean we will become slave traders in all but name. We will open up whole sections of the South to them."

"I know what it will mean," Gertrude said. "Tell them anyway."

There was the sound of a door shutting, and Gertrude looked into another corner of the room.

"When it is done, Poull will have to die," she said. "His heart is too soft for this, and he knows too much of our business."

Kate watched it, not wanting to believe any of it. Siobhan could be making this up. It could be an illusion projected onto the water.

"You know that it is true though, don't you?" Siobhan said. "You have a measure of talent for it, and you can feel that it is real. If I hadn't need of a warrior, I could have trained you as a seer."

Kate wanted to believe that it was a lie, but honestly, why *would* Siobhan lie about this? She didn't have to give Kate a reason for the things she'd ordered her to do. She didn't have to pretend that Gertrude would have turned out like this.

"She takes up her father's business," Siobhan says. "And in his memory, she discovers a determination to succeed, whatever it takes."

"And so she becomes something evil?" Kate said.

"I told you before that the world is rarely so simple," Siobhan said. "But yes, she becomes cruel. She causes more harm than good in the world. Not all at once, of course. It starts with a letter that must be forged first to keep control of the business, then men who must be blackmailed or bribed. A rival must be murdered, because the alternative is being condemned for all she has done already. It happens step by step, until a monster hurts thousands, tens of thousands, for her profits."

Kate could imagine it happening. She'd seen how easily people could be enticed to do cruel or evil things, simply because it was in their interest to do it. Even so, it was hard to know what to think.

"She was still innocent *now*," Kate said.

"She was," Siobhan agreed. "But how many people should we wait for her to hurt before we act? Should we wait until she ruins her first life? Until she kills her first foe? Doing it now means that her father is heartbroken. He still dies, but he breaks up his business first, trying to do the good that he thinks she would have wanted him to do. Wait a while, and even that will not happen."

Siobhan made it all seem so logical and so straightforward. Kill Gertrude, and her evil did not happen, while good happened instead. Kill her, and Kate made the world a better place.

"And you still threatened to kill my sister," Kate pointed out. She couldn't forgive that. She wouldn't.

"Did I?" Siobhan said. "I said that she would die. I said that you could make the choice. Did it not occur to you that if Gertrude Illiard had lived, her affairs might brush up against someone like Sophia, roll over her, *crush* her?"

"You're saying she would have killed my sister?" Kate asked.

Siobhan laughed at that. "Oh, you're still thinking far too simplistically. Effects are not a single set of ripples, spreading out from a rock. They are a handful of pebbles all thrown at once, the ripples bouncing from one another. But you chose, and that is all that matters."

"You picked this woman deliberately, didn't you?" Kate said. "You want to use me in this game of consequences you're playing, so you picked this to get me to trust that you would make the right choices."

Siobhan smiled at that. "So wise for one so young. Or so foolish. It's hard to tell with your kind, sometimes."

"You've only made one mistake," Kate pointed out.

Siobhan stood there, obviously waiting for Kate to continue. She didn't seem worried by it. She should have been.

"You sent me to do this as my favor to you," Kate said. She turned on her heel. "I don't owe you anything anymore."

She expected Siobhan to be angry then, to try to pull her back. She almost hoped that she would attack, so that Kate had an excuse to use the blade at her hip. Siobhan might show her the place where she kept the souls of those who broke their deals, but Kate had *kept* her bargain.

Instead, though, she heard Siobhan laugh.

"Oh, do you think it's that simple?" she asked. "Do your favor and walk away?"

"I've done what you wanted," Kate said. "I'm free."

Siobhan kept laughing. "Until next time, apprentice."

Kate could hear the claim in that last word. She set off walking. "No," she insisted. "I'm free."

"You'll never be free," Siobhan said. "Do you think there's any action you take I won't influence? Do you think that the next time I ask you for something, you won't do it? *Do you think you get to walk away from me?*"

The brambles slashed at her, and Kate ran.

She sprinted through the woods, ignoring the cuts that appeared on her arms and legs, ducking and rolling to avoid a branch that seemed to swing toward her too fast for the wind. She sprinted through the mud and the fallen leaves of the forest floor, dodging around trees, not slowing, because it felt as though even slowing would draw her back.

She'd done her part. She wouldn't be Siobhan's plaything. She wouldn't kill and kill at the forest woman's command. She wouldn't be a mindless weapon to be wielded like a gardener's shears by someone trying to shape the strands of the future.

So she ran. When a branch came too close, Kate hacked it down with her sword and kept going. When bramble bushes filled the path ahead, Kate leapt over them, rolling as she landed. She ran until she saw the edge of the wood and sprinted out into the light.

She'd done it. She was clear. She was free.

Then she heard Siobhan's voice, her laughter drifting on the wind.

"Do you really think it's that easy, Kate? You will never truly be free. We're bound together now, and some things *cannot* be undone."

CHAPTER ELEVEN

When they reached the estate, Sophia stood staring at the great house at its heart. It was huge and crenulated, halfway to being the kind of castle that had meant something, back before cannon had been able to bring down walls and shatter fortified gateways.

The estate looked as though it had found it out the hard way. The hills around it would have provided some protection, but even so, whole sections of it were ruined, one wing reduced to little more than rubble. There were scorch marks on the outside where fire had claimed portions of it, while the grounds were overgrown with brambles and long grass. Even so, she stared at it

"What is it?" Cora asked.

"It's a long way to come for a wreck," Emeline said.

Sophia shook her head. "I've seen this before. I know this place."

She walked down toward it with Sienne and the others in her wake. She crossed over lawns that were little more than tangled squares of grass, sorely in need of a gardener's scythe. Ahead, there were great, iron-bound doors that proved to be shut tight when Sophia tried them, but a window nearby was broken and empty of glass.

"You're just going to climb in?" Cora asked, as Sophia started to clamber through. "What if there's someone inside?"

"I don't think there is," she said. "This whole place just looks dead."

She couldn't keep the disappointment out of her voice at that. When she'd set off here, she'd been hoping for a bustling home still filled with people. A part of her had even dared to hope that maybe her parents might be there, whatever everyone else had said. Even as she'd known it couldn't be true, that they were long dead, she'd hoped.

There was no one here for her, though, just an empty shell of a building, filled with cobwebs. Sophia brushed some aside as she climbed in through the window, hopping lightly into a room that probably had been a bright and happy place once. The furniture had the opulence of rich woods and fine silks, while the ornaments shone with flashes of gold. A chandelier above looked as though it hadn't been lit in years, but it still shone with crystal and silver.

Now, it seemed still and leached of all color, a layer of dust lending a corpselike pallor to wood and cloth, leather and metal alike.

"At least we'll be out of the cold tonight," Emeline said, her tone obviously already dismissing the great house as anything more.

This was Monthys House, though, and Sophia knew as the name came to her that the place had been named like that rather than with a family name because its owners had wanted to emphasize their connection to the lands around them. The very fact that she could remember that told her that she'd found the right place. She could remember how beautiful it had been, and maybe could be again. It wouldn't take much to get a fire going in the grate, and even the cobwebs could be chased away with enough effort.

"I know this house," Sophia insisted. "I've been here before. I've been in this room."

The memories were there, just below the surface, there every time she reached in by looking at an object or taking in the pattern of light a familiar window made on the floor. Sophia went over to a portrait of a woman in clothes that suggested it had been painted hundreds of years before. Sophia could remember looking at this painting as a small child, wondering why her mother was wearing such a funny costume.

"She looks like you," Emeline said, and that seemed to be enough to catch her interest. "This place really is your family's, isn't it?"

"I think so," Sophia said. "And she... I think she's one of my ancestors."

"And this is your great-great-great-great-grandmother, girls," Anora said.

Sophia tried to repeat it back to her, but her nurse laughed.

"Not enough greats. Still, we'll get there. You should know your family, girls. You should know who you are."

"Can we play outside yet?" Kate had asked. "Can we play throwing stones?"

The memory came back to Sophia with a sharpness that felt as though it might have happened yesterday. There were more memories as her fingers traced along a table, finding a plate Kate had almost broken jumping around, a crack in the wall that she could remember looking into when she was small, assuming that there might be whole worlds in there.

"Come on," she said. "I need to see this."

She needed it like an itch she couldn't scratch, like a hunger that had been sitting in her belly for so long she had ceased to notice it until there was finally the opportunity for a feast. Now she was ravenous for what she might learn, the sheer need for memory overwhelming everything else as she set off out of the room, turning left, then right along corridors by instinct. The walls were familiar, paneled with woods that had been brought from all the lands their family had visited: dark ebony and blood-red satine, pale maple and deep brown oak, all exquisitely carved with scenes showing monsters and plants and foreign lands and strange figures.

She found a low grate, and her hands moved surely to pull it out of the way, revealing a tiny space behind it that had been left by the creation of a new wing a generation before.

"Kate and I used to hide in here from our nurse," Sophia said. "We used to play hide and seek all over the house."

She could still find the spots where they'd hidden from one another, and then later from the men who'd come to the house. She could remember hiding with Anora at first, and then later the nurse's screams when the men had nearly found them.

"Run, girls!" she'd hissed to them. "I'll draw them off. I... I love you both."

She made her way through the empty rooms of the house, looking around at so many reminders of the past that it seemed wherever she glanced there were fresh memories waiting for her. The house looked different, smaller than she remembered it, but Sophia guessed that had been because she'd been so much younger when she'd seen it last.

She led the way into a long gallery, filled with paintings of ancestors Anora had tried to teach them, set in frames of gold and dark wood. For the moment, Sophia walked past them all, focusing on a larger painting toward the end. It drew her in, even though it was so covered in cobwebs that Sophia couldn't see the image that lay beneath.

Gently, using the cloth of her sleeve, she started to wipe away the patina that had built up over all of it. She didn't want to risk disturbing the oils, but she needed to see what lay underneath the grime. It gave way reluctantly, but Sophia kept going, slowly revealing what lay beneath. When she was done, she stood back, and she could feel tears starting to sting her eyes.

She stood there in the painting, or a younger version of her at least. Kate was with her, holding onto her hand with an expression that said she would rather have been running around the gardens than standing there being painted. Behind them stood the man and woman Sophia knew from the painting Laurette van Klet had shown her. From her dreams.

"My parents," Sophia said, managing to choke back a sob.

"*These* are your parents?" Cora said. She stepped forward to wipe away the dust from a small plaque below the painting.

Alfred, Christina, Sophia, and Kate of the House of Danse.

"Danse?" Emeline said, and Sophia could hear the catch in her voice. "I knew your parents were someone important when you started talking about their estates, but *this*? You're one of the Danses?"

Sophia didn't understand the shock in her voice, but right then, she was concentrating on other things. She moved along the line of paintings in the gallery, looking at men and women whose portraits she already knew because she'd spent rainy afternoons in this room, listening to her nursemaid telling stories about them.

This is Lady Sophia, you're named after her. She persuaded the Mountain Lands to join themselves to the kingdom, at least in name.

Sophia stared at a portrait of a woman who reminded her a little of Kate, with that same determination in her eyes, and a sense of the same restless energy.

This is Lady Denana, who fought off an invasion of troll folk in the mist years.

Every painting had a story attached to it, a moment in history, or a connection between families. *Her* family. That was the part that was proving hard to accept. All of these people, this endless string of paintings, represented links in a chain that led to Sophia and her sister. She didn't know what to make of it all, even with the memories that came to her with the sight of every face there.

"You're really one of the Danses?" Emeline said.

Sophia shrugged. "I... guess so?"

"But that's... that's *incredible*."

Sophia frowned, looking around at her. "I don't understand. What's so special about it?"

Emeline looked a little shocked by that. "You don't know who they were? No, I guess you might not."

"It isn't something they talk about openly," Cora said. "Around the court, even mentioning them was enough to get you punished. I saw a man taken away by the guards just because he expressed sympathy for what happened to them."

That was a big thing. The kingdom, with its Assembly of Nobles, supposedly kept people safe from that kind of arbitrary arrest. If it happened anyway, it suggested that it was something too dangerous to touch. Sophia found herself thinking of what the artist Laurette van Klet had told her.

"I heard that they were close to the throne before the civil wars," Sophia said.

Emeline laughed at that. "Close to it? They *held* the throne before the first one. They ruled us, but there were nobles who weren't satisfied with them, with how close they got to the magic of the kingdom, or with how they treated the people who had that magic. Do you know what the civil wars were *about?*"

Sophia shrugged. "At the orphanage, they said the crown argued with the nobles about how much power it should have."

"And that's it?" Emeline said. She sighed. "They've tried to wipe you out of history. I mean, it's true, but it's not even close to everything. The *first* move in the civil wars came when the House of Flamberg took the throne from the House of Danse about a century ago."

That was a long time for a war. Emeline must have caught some of what Sophia was thinking, because she shook her head.

"I don't mean that it happened all at once. It's like... you know how the wars across the Knifewater are big and complicated and there are about a hundred different sides?"

"Or there were," Cora said. "Before this New Army."

Sophia nodded.

"It was that complicated with the civil wars here too," Emeline said. "The Danses kind of held things together, they had a kind of connection to the land, the magic that came from it. Once the Flambergs took over, all of it came to the surface. There were those who were jealous. The Church of the Masked Goddess said that magic was evil. The nobles wanted power for themselves. There were arguments about whether the Indentured should be free."

"So there was a war," Cora said.

"There were *wars*," Emeline corrected her. "A century of petty rebellions and wars. They gave us the Assembly of Nobles, the Masked Goddess's church, the death of the king leaving the Dowager and her sons."

"And the murder of my parents," Sophia said, feeling the pain of that night all over again. She'd seen the danger of it all in her dreams. She could *remember* running through this house, knowing that there were men who would have killed her if they'd managed to find her. "They wanted to kill me too."

"Because you're the Danses' eldest daughter," Cora said. "You... you're the heir to the throne."

"There are those who would say you were, anyway," Emeline said. "Technically, your family accepted being made just nobles, but there were always those who wanted to rally behind them and put them back in place." She shrugged. "Maybe things *would* have been better if they never left the throne. Maybe not. It's hard to see how they could be much worse."

It was too much. She'd picked the connection to the throne from Laurette van Klet's mind, but she hadn't really understood how real it was. She definitely hadn't understood what it had meant for her, or how it had brought about the terrible things that lived in her memory. Her family had been attacked for who they were as much as for anything they'd done. She'd met the Dowager, and she could imagine Sebastian's mother seeing the threat there all too easily.

That understanding hurt, but Sophia pushed past it. She wasn't just here for the past. She was looking for any information about the present, too. Her parents had told her to run and hide, said that they would try to meet up with her. Sophia had seen the scale of the violence that night, but someone had to have survived besides her and Kate, didn't they? Maybe they'd left a sign.

There were hidden places in the house. Sophia knew all of them, because she and Kate had made a game of trying to find all the spots that had been hidden or simply forgotten. There was the room hidden behind a bookcase, the cupboard-sized hole beneath a series of floorboards.

"A hiding place for the Indentured for when they sent hunters after them," Emeline guessed. "Even your ancestors couldn't just declare people free. Some evils stick too well for that."

Sophia could feel the pain behind that. She couldn't blame Emeline. This was a cruel world, which seemed almost determined to stamp on the weak. She didn't answer, though, because in that moment, she'd remembered another hiding place. She hurried through to a sitting room where the furniture looked as though it hadn't been touched in years. There were even wine glasses on the table, with liquid in them that had long since turned to vinegar.

Sophia went over to a panel on the wall. She'd seen her father do this once, watching with delight as he'd touched it *here* and *here*. The memory came back to her so clearly that for a moment Sophia could imagine she was him as her hands followed the movements his had made.

A click sounded, sharp as a crossbow, and the panel swung back to reveal a cabinet-sized space. Inside, a tightly rolled sheaf of paper sat waiting, as it had presumably been waiting all these years.

CHAPTER TWELVE

It took a while for Kate to calm down enough to realize that she couldn't keep running forever. Running blindly didn't make anything better. Worse, it meant that she was still reacting to Siobhan, still doing whatever the woman of the forest wanted her to do. She forced herself to walk, forced herself to think.

Then she headed back in the direction of the training grounds and Lord Cranston's regiment.

Kate *could* have headed for the forge, but she didn't, for a couple of reasons. One was that if Siobhan sent any kind of trouble after her, the soldiers would be better equipped to deal with it than Thomas and Winifred were. Another was that she had to go back to the regiment at some point, or they would come looking for her for desertion. Lord Cranston had given her some slack in the wake of the victory over the invaders, but Kate suspected that she was rapidly burning through it. Even the free companies maintained their discipline. Maybe *especially* the free companies, because no one wanted undisciplined mercenaries doing what they wanted around the kingdom.

So she walked back to the training grounds, and by the time she returned there, the other members of the company were already gathered back there from whatever time they'd spent celebrating in the city. They had the lazy look of men recovering from heads too thick with drink, but at least when Kate walked past them, they looked at her with a measure of respect now.

Will was with the group of artillerists who worked with him on the cannon, scrubbing it down and getting it ready for use. He ran over to her as she approached, throwing his arms around her. Kate wished that she could kiss him in that moment, but she suspected that would just bring her jeers from the others there, and in any case, there were things she didn't want to do in front of so many others.

"You came back," he said, and Kate could feel the relief there. From his thoughts, she could see that he wanted to kiss her as much as she did him. "I always worry that you won't when you go off like that."

67

Kate could see him imagining a life where she didn't wander off, doing dangerous things; where they could both be safe and happy in a home of their own. Kate wished that she could promise him something like that, but the truth was that it wasn't the life she was cut out for. It just wasn't who she was.

"You need to get to Lord Cranston," Will said, lowering his voice. "He left word with me to send you over as soon as you came."

Which meant he'd expected her to go to Will first, and that he had something that he needed doing. Probably the usual combination of chore and test.

"What is it?" Kate asked. "Does he want me to take his socks to be darned while dodging arrows? Recite the commanders of city states' armies while cleaning his armor?"

"I think it's more serious than that," Will said. "The others are talking about another messenger from the Dowager. You know how rumors spread."

Kate did. She also knew that the last time there had been a messenger like that, they'd ended up fighting to defend the shores of the kingdom from attack. There was no time to waste, so she ran through the camp, dodging around soldiers even as they tried to congratulate her on her role in their last victory.

By the time she came sprinting up to Lord Cranston's tent, Kate was out of breath. The company's commander stood there looking like a slightly ragged fop, the gray in his mustache and hair dyed out with oil. His clothes had probably been the finest money could buy at one time, but now had discreet patches and stitching to hold them together.

There was another man there, and Kate recognized him from the last time the Dowager had sent a messenger. It was true then; their company was to go into battle again.

"Ah, Kate," Lord Cranston said as she approached. "You're just in time. Our friend here has just been congratulating us on our role in repulsing the New Army's men."

"He's here to congratulate us?" Kate said. She didn't believe it, and not just because the camp would have been in a far more ebullient mood if it had been the case. Rulers, she suspected, didn't show gratitude unless they wanted something.

One glance at the messenger's thoughts told her the truth of it.

"And to ask us to fight again," Kate added.

"Indeed," Lord Cranston said, and his tone was tight. "Although 'ask' is probably a strong word for it." He handed over a sheet of parchment.

68

As a result of the incursion of foreign forces onto our shores, the Assembly requires all companies of armed men within the kingdom to mobilize and make themselves available under the command of the rightfully appointed officers of Her Majesty, to...

Kate didn't need to read more than that to get the gist of it. "They're commanding us to do what the Dowager wants. Can they do that?"

Lord Cranston nodded. "With an instruction from the Assembly, they can."

"And we have to go where they want? Fight who they say we fight?" Kate asked. She could feel how unhappy Lord Cranston was at this, just as she could pick up the gloating satisfaction of the messenger. Maybe she shouldn't have driven such a hard bargain with him the first time he'd come to the camp.

"Failure to obey would be seen as desertion or aiding the enemy," the messenger said. "I must inform you that articles for your arrest would then be drafted, enforceable with the aid of other regiments, if necessary."

He tried to make it sound like an unfortunate possibility, but Kate could see how much he wanted it to come to that.

"And we still get paid for this?" Kate asked.

Lord Cranston smiled a little at that. "Still asking the right questions, at least. Look further down the instructions."

Payment for free companies is to be at the rate of regular soldiers, held one month in arrears.

That stoked Kate's anger a little, although not because she particularly cared about the money. It was more because she knew how much Lord Cranston *would* care, and because of what it would mean for everyone in the company, including Will.

"Is this some kind of punishment?" Kate asked with a frown.

"A punishment?" the messenger said. "It is no more than a necessity of war. The kingdom can afford to employ free companies on an ad hoc basis at other times, but with the current threat, there simply isn't the coin."

Kate shook her head. "I don't believe you. This is about something else. What?"

The messenger took a step back as she moved toward him.

"What makes you think I have any answers for you?"

His thoughts betrayed him, though. *If you weren't here, there would be no need for this. This is what Lord Cranston gets for taking on murderers.*

69

That thought slid into Kate like a knife. This was because she was there? After all she'd done to help on the beach, they were still going to punish the whole company she was in like this?

She looked over to Lord Cranston. "I'm so sorry, I'm—"

He held up a hand to cut her off. "Not in front of our guest, please, Kate. Besides, we still have to hear the details of what he wants done. I take it that there *is* a specific task that Her Majesty has in mind?"

Kate could see the shape of it in the messenger's mind like a looming boulder about to topple on them.

"Given your previous success against the New Army," the messenger said, "it was felt that your company might be the right choice to take the fight to the enemy. That is why I have orders for you to attack the Port of Carrick, where it is believed many of the enemy's ships are moored. You will destroy as many of the ships as possible, damage their supplies, and take any other steps possible to reduce their opportunities for the invasion of our island."

He held out another piece of paper, and this one was sealed with the Dowager's crest. Kate had no doubt that it would say the same things the messenger had just taken such amusement in telling them. Lord Cranston reached out to take the paper with a formal bow.

"Thank you for your message," he said. "Please inform our queen that we remain her dutiful servants."

"Of course," the messenger said. "Your transport ships will be waiting for you at the docks on the morning tide."

"Thank you," Lord Cranston. "Now, please leave my camp before I feel the need to put a musket ball in your skull."

He said that in the same polite, formal tone that he'd used before, but Kate could see that he was serious about the threat. Apparently, so could the messenger. The man returned Lord Cranston's bow in a hurry, then sped off through the camp, back in the direction of Ashton.

"He'll report that you threatened him," Kate pointed out.

Lord Cranston shrugged. "Men like him will always find someone to chatter to. It rarely makes a difference to the world, and in any case, I am likely to be dead long before anything comes of it."

"Dead?" Kate asked.

She could feel the pall of depression that had sunk over Lord Cranston now like some low-lying fog. His thoughts were filled with violence, but for once, they weren't about the simple practicalities involved, or the joy of outthinking a foe. No, he was

70

thinking about what it would be like to die in battle, and for his grand adventure as a mercenary to come to an end.

"Yes, Kate, dead," Lord Cranston said. "Dead, and for what? A soldier's wages?" He spat like a common soldier. "It's almost enough to make a man want to find a better side to fight for. A more lucrative one, at least."

Kate could see that he didn't mean it, but just the fact that he was willing to say it said something about the situation they faced.

"Exactly how bad is it?" Kate asked.

Lord Cranston gestured for her to follow him. "There is at least an opportunity for another lesson here. Come with me."

He led the way to his tent, where he pulled out a book from the great iron-bound chest that seemed to hold almost everything he owned. Kate knew from other times spent looking at it that it contained map after map, some representing far-off parts of the world, some setting out the way long-ago battles had unfolded.

"This is the Third Battle of Carrick, about twenty years ago," Lord Cranston said. "In it, an invading force three times the size of the defending contingent assaulted the city. They were slaughtered."

"But the New Army took the city," Kate insisted. "There must be a chance."

Lord Cranston shook his head. "They took it through treachery, when the men of Carrick heard the Master of Crows' reputation and decided that his coin was preferable to the alternatives. Unless you can think of a way for us to outbid him now, I think we are being sent to be waves breaking on the shore."

"Why?" Kate asked. "Why would anyone do that in a war? Why would they send their own forces out to die when we could be doing something useful to protect the coast?"

Lord Cranston spread his hands. "It could be jealousy, that we succeeded in a battle that should have been the royal regiments'. It could be fear that, buoyed by our success, we might try to act against the crown. It might even be some jealous noble from my past, because I bedded a few men's wives when I was younger."

"You don't think it's any of that, though," Kate said. It wasn't a question, because she could see that Lord Cranston wasn't thinking that way. "You think it's about me."

Lord Cranston hesitated, as if he might lie about it, but then nodded.

"What else can it be? I take in a girl who has just slain an orphanage full of masked nuns, and my men are sent out to battle. We succeed in that, and we're sent out again, to a fight that no one could expect to win. If I were a sensible man I would have hanged you when I had the chance."

He said it in a friendly tone, but Kate could see that he wasn't entirely joking. Sparing her life was about to cost Lord Cranston his, along with those of most of his men. Kate could hardly blame him, looked at like that.

"So, what do we do?" she asked.

"What *can* we do?" Lord Cranston countered. "You ask me that as if I have some cunning plan stored away for moments when my queen and country decide that they would be better off without me."

"And don't you?" Kate replied.

Lord Cranston paused. "Well, yes, but it mostly involves running with whatever gold I have and retiring to a nice sunny island somewhere, and *that* would involve abandoning my men. I'll not do it. Not here, not now."

It was a curious degree of loyalty from a man who claimed to mostly be motivated by the money he could make from war. It made Kate think about her own loyalties.

"I could leave," Kate said. "You could let it be known that you aren't protecting me."

Lord Cranston shook his head. "These orders have been given. Besides, I will *not* have this done to me, only to give up my student."

"So what do we do, then?" Kate asked.

"What else is there to do?" Lord Cranston shot back. "We fight. We're going to go to a city that hasn't been taken and try to destroy the fleet carrying an army that can't be beaten. All I can say is that, when we die in the attempt, they had better sing songs about my efforts."

CHAPTER THIRTEEN

With trembling hands, Sophia took the papers from the hidden space behind the panel. The square of a letter was sealed with blank wax and had her name written on it in a hurried script, the ink long since dry. She held it up to the light, looking for any clue to who had left it, and why.

The answer to the first part of it was obvious though. There were only a few people who knew about the existence of this compartment. If everyone knew, it would have been emptied long ago. That meant... that meant that this letter was from her parents, to her. She saw a matching one with Kate's name and took it, tucking it away inside her dress unread. The one for herself, she took over to a table, staring at it as she tried to imagine all the things that might lie within.

"Why don't you just open it?" Emeline said with a hint of impatience.

"Shh," Cora hissed back. "Can't you see how difficult this is for her? For someone who can see everyone's thoughts, you don't have a lot of empathy sometimes."

Sophia ignored them both, concentrating on the feel of the vellum under her fingers, the unmarked wax sealing it. Emeline was right, of course; without opening it, she couldn't know what lay within. Her fingers found the wax and broke it open with a snap, the brittle material giving way with the ease of age.

The paper was stiff, and so delicate that now Sophia didn't dare bring it out into the light in case it crumbled to nothing under the strength of the sun's rays. She shielded it with her body as she unfolded it carefully, the square turning into a larger sheet, filled with neat, bold writing. She didn't even know if it was her father's hand or her mother's, but she started reading anyway.

My beautiful daughter,

If you are reading this, then you have returned to our family home, and we are not there. I can only imagine the things that you must have been through in the meantime, and both my heart and

73

your father's break with the thought that we couldn't all be together.

This was her mother's writing then. Sophia touched it, feeling a small flash of pain at finally being able to connect the woman she saw in her dreams to words that weren't remembered ones. She kept reading.

I cannot say where we are now, because I do not know where we will be by the time you read this. Perhaps you will be reading it at a point when we have already found you, or perhaps you will not have seen us from the night when we were riven apart. I dare not guess, either, because to do so would be to give away too many safe places to our enemies in the event that they find this letter.

Sophia could feel her heart breaking with those words. She'd come here to find her parents and her heritage. She'd hoped that it would all be perfect once she got here; that she would find a vibrant, welcoming home from which she could send for her sister. Instead, she'd found an empty building, and a letter that wouldn't even tell her where to look next.

There are things that I can tell you, though. First, remember who you are and why this is happening. You are the eldest child of the last generation of Danses. In another time, you would have been the heir to the kingdom's throne, and more than that. You would have been the living heart of the kingdom, joined to it in a way that the Flambergs can never be, whatever they claim for themselves and their goddess.

That confirmed the things Sophia had already guessed, looking at the paintings, but it went further, too. It hinted at things Sophia wasn't sure she understood. How could someone be the heart of the kingdom? She remembered what Emeline had hinted at before.

"What did you mean, that my family had a magical connection to the kingdom?" Sophia asked her.

Emeline spread her hands. "I don't know the details," she said. "It was always just a story from before I was born, and one you couldn't tell where there was any risk that a priest or a spy might hear it."

Sophia could understand that. She was asking the other girl questions about something she'd probably never paid any attention

74

to, because what effect did any of this have on her life? Even so, Sophia had to know.

"Please," she said. "Anything you can remember might help."

"I don't know," Emeline said. "I think the idea was that the kingdom was almost like some kind of living thing, and they could keep it healthy. I'm sorry, I didn't really pay attention."

"No, I understand," Sophia said. In any case it seemed too incredible to believe. She knew the limits of her powers, or she thought that she did, anyway. She could read minds, and connect to people at a distance. Apparently, she could influence the mind of an animal like Sienne, who curled against her legs even now. She couldn't control an entire kingdom.

There was more to the letter, though:

In this compartment, you will find family trees showing who you are. Your uncle, my brother, is Lars Skyddar. Unless things have changed more than I could believe, he and his family rule in the ice lands around Ausberg. The docks to the east of Monthys have always had traders from Ishjemme. They should be able to get you to the city. If you can reach him, I believe that you will be safe. His army is a powerful one, and the ice has always been a deterrent to invaders.

There it was, another step in the long chain of them that Sophia hoped would lead her and her sister to safety. She wanted to believe that it was true. More than that, she wanted to believe that this might finally give them a chance to find their parents.

Your uncle will be able to vouch for who you are. I cannot think what your life will have been like apart from us, but he will allow you to reclaim who you are. If you wish to do it, he may be able to help you reclaim the kingdom that should always have been yours. Your father and I chose not to push our claims for the throne, because we thought it would bring peace in the wake of the civil wars. The truth was that it made things no better. It let the Flambergs do as they wished. Perhaps the time has come for that to stop.

Sophia didn't know what to make of that. Did her mother really think that she would be in a position to take the kingdom from the Dowager? Did she think that Sophia would want to restart the civil wars?

75

The scariest part of the thought was the possibility that she might be able to do it. Just the idea that she was someone who could walk up and make a claim to the throne was… it felt insane. It would have been enough to learn that she had a living relative, an uncle she could go to. To learn that uncle was the ruler of his own land felt like too much. To hear that he might have an army to lend her to take her own kingdom… it was beyond anything Sophia could take in.

Whatever happens, know that we did not part from you willingly. My hope is that Lars will be able to give you everything you should have ever had, while my shame is that we were not able to be there to do it. Know that we love you, and we have always loved you. Everything we did was from that love, even leaving you. I hope you find a way to be safe. I love you.
Your Mother

That was all of it. Sophia turned the paper over in case there might be more, and when she turned it back, she could see the wet marks of her tears on the paper. It felt as though reading this, finally finding some connection to her mother, had opened a gate within her, and the tears fell through.

Cora and Emeline both put their arms around her, holding her close. Sophia appreciated the gesture, but it just brought back thoughts of being held by her parents, the memories bringing fresh pain with them. She'd expected so much from her journey to her parents' home, but this was both too much and too little, all at once.

It was too much, because some of the things she'd learned during her time here seemed impossible to take in. On one level, Sophia could understand all the talk of her connection to royalty, and the thought that she might be the rightful heir to the throne. Yet, when it came to actually imagining herself in that position, she simply couldn't do it.

It was too little, because whatever else this journey had given her, it hadn't given Sophia her parents back. She didn't know where they were. She didn't even know what had happened to them, or when this letter had been put there. She'd been hoping that they would be waiting there at the house, or at least that there would be a way to get to them from there. Instead, there had been no more than memories and a letter that told her no more.

Sophia was still trying to find a way through the muddle of thoughts when a crash came from somewhere above them. She stepped back from her friends, looking up in the direction the sound had come from.

"There's someone here," she said.

"But I thought this place was empty," Cora replied.

Sophia had thought the same. She hadn't been able to feel the presence of another mind there, but the truth was that she wasn't certain she would have even if there were someone there.

"It can be hard to sense people consistently," Emeline said, answering her unspoken question. "Maybe there was someone hiding."

Cora looked worried by that prospect. "Should we find out who it is?" she asked. "What if they're dangerous?"

It was a risk, but with Sienne by her side, Sophia felt relatively safe there. She wanted to find this person, whoever they were. Perhaps they knew more than was contained in the few scraps of paper the hidden compartment had held.

Perhaps they knew what had happened to her parents.

"I want to find them," she said, and led the way through the house, trusting that the others would follow. They did, Sienne padding along beside her while Cora and Emeline followed in her wake.

More sounds came from above, and Sophia knew that she needed to find some stairs if she was going to locate whoever was moving around. And it was a person, she was sure of it now. She could feel the presence of a set of thoughts, and it didn't feel like an animal, even if, at this distance, she didn't feel as though she could read them to find out who this was.

Her memory supplied her with a route to a set of servants' stairs, there so that servants could make their way through the great house without getting in the way of any guests. She and Kate had liked to run through hidden places like that when they were small, and their parents had let them, saying that the idea that servants should be hidden away was nonsense.

Sophia made her way up them now. The wood creaked under her feet in a way that suggested it was as poorly maintained as some of the rest of the house. She crept upstairs with the others, looking for whoever was up there.

On this level, she could see more signs of the fire, and of violence. There were soot stains on the walls, and gaps in the roof that let in a view of the sky. There were dark stains on the wood that at first she thought might be more soot, but that closer examination revealed to be blood. Sophia's memory supplied the screams of servants as she and Kate had hidden. That night had been a thing of cruelty and thoughtless violence. Sophia didn't want to think about it.

She needed to concentrate on the figure she'd sensed. She'd lost track of them now, but she knew roughly where they'd been: ahead, in the quarters reserved for the cook and the butler, the head gardener, and the other key members of the household. Sophia crept forward, wondering what she would find ahead.

Sophia heard Sienne growl then, in a low voice that spoke of the possibility of danger. She was learning to trust the forest cat's instincts by now, and she spun, looking for danger.

"Hold!" a voice said. "Who goes there?"

There was a figure ahead, little more than a silhouette in the light from the broken roof section. Even like that, though, Sophia could see the crossbow in the figure's hands, leveled at her heart.

"Tell me who you are!" the figure called. "Or I'll kill you all like the thieves you are!"

CHAPTER FOURTEEN

Kate had never sailed before, and she should have been enraptured with the excitement of the new experience. She should have spent her time running to all corners of the transport ship, from the lowest bilges to the top of the crows' nest. She should have at least been able to spend the journey over with Will, finding a quiet space somewhere to be together.

Instead, she spent the journey to Carrick consumed with a mixture of dread and guilt.

The dread came from the tension that was running through all the men on the ship. In such a confined space, Kate's power could reach out almost at random and find a dozen men worrying about the tales of Carrick's impregnability, or the stories of the Master of Crows' talent for war. Even Lord Cranston seemed to be filled with it, his thoughts spinning with half-formed plans that only seemed to be depressing him with their ineffectiveness. He'd snapped at Kate several times on the way over, and the sheer incongruity of that had shown her just how terrifying this was.

The guilt was simpler: this was all her fault. She could see *that* thought in the minds of the men around her too, although at least some of them tried to hide it. She didn't need to see it to know it was true. This was happening as a way to punish Lord Cranston for having her in his regiment. It wouldn't have happened if Kate hadn't joined his troops, hadn't insisted on beating his sword master.

If she weren't there, Lord Cranston, and his men, and Will would be safe.

But it was too late to do anything about that. It wasn't as though she could leave the company while they were still at sea, short of jumping over the side and hoping that she washed ashore somewhere better.

Even if she'd wanted to do that, there was no time for it, because the Dowager had picked fast ships to transport Lord Cranston's company. Carrick was already coming into view, in a wide swath of stone, wood, metal, and sand.

"Look at it, Kate," Lord Cranston said, handing over an eyeglass. "Look at it and tell me what you see."

Kate took the eyeglass and stared at the city ahead. The only city Kate had known was Ashton, and this was *nothing* like Ashton. Where the capital of the Dowager's kingdom sprawled well past its walls in a flat wash of buildings, Carrick was contained in them like the fortress it was. Worse, Kate could see that those walls weren't ancient things of simple stone, easily blown through with cannon. There were redoubts and sand banks there, palisades and extended lines of defenses.

"It really is a fortress," Kate said.

"But one that we are obliged to attack," Lord Cranston replied. "The fleet there is gathering."

Kate could see it, an armada of vessels that seemed to range from cogs to galleons, their sails furled as they sat ready to be supplied with soldiers and weapons. It was obvious that they were readying for an invasion. It was just as obvious that anyone trying to assault the city would do so in the face of a storm of lead shot and cannon fire.

"It's a death trap," Kate said.

"There are things that a commander doesn't say," Lord Cranston replied.

"Not even 'this is a bad idea, let's regroup and try something else'?" Kate suggested.

Lord Cranston shook his head at that. "Not if that commander wants to avoid angering his queen, in this case. We have to attack."

Kate couldn't see how it could happen. If they dove into the midst of all that, they would die. The enemy would sweep around them like water around a drowning man and slaughter their entire company.

"How?" she asked. "I can't see a way."

She could see the uncertainty in Lord Cranston's thoughts too, but he didn't show it on the outside. "We'll go in along the beach line, run in, and try to attack by surprise. Once we get there, we try to fire as many ships as we can in the first few seconds and make a grab for one of their standards. That is vital. Then we run, and we hope that we can run fast enough."

Kate could understand the idea of hitting and running against something that seemed so impregnable. There was one part that she didn't understand.

"Why is a standard so important?" she asked.

"Because we have to remember our goal here is not the defeat of the Master of Crows' army," Lord Cranston said.

Kate frowned at that. "It isn't?"

"No." Lord Cranston took his eyeglass back and closed it with a snap. "Our goal is to find a way to provide the Assembly of Nobles with proof that we have complied with the Dowager's orders. People have the stupid idea that seizing a standard from a company is a great feat of bravery, and so we will provide them with that proof of our daring raid. I just hope it will be enough."

Kate vowed silently that if she could get Lord Cranston the standard he wanted, she would. For now, there was nothing to do but wait, watching the swirl of the seabirds overhead. Was there the darker flicker of crow feathers among them?

They came in close to shore, and now the company disembarked, wading through the shallow water. Kate went with them, moving swiftly and quietly.

"I think I saw crows," she whispered to Lord Cranston. "They know we're coming."

He nodded, but didn't answer. Kate guessed that there was nothing to say. They still had to do this.

"Attack!" he called, waving his men forward. "Quickly now! Raiding parties!"

His men surged forward along the beach, and perhaps their speed saved some of them as the first cannon fire roared across the approach to Carrick's docks. Sand flew up in great gouts, and for a moment Kate couldn't see anything of the world around her. That didn't matter though. Right then, the only option was to keep moving forward.

She heard her ship's cannons firing in response to the assault, and she thought of Will. Would he be safe, there on the ship, or would it just make him a sitting target in the violence? The worst part was that there was nothing Kate could do to keep him safe, nothing that she could do about any of the chaos around her. This was the reality of war: it didn't matter how great her skills as a warrior were, because death could come from nowhere in an instant.

She saw the truth of that as men were brought down by musket balls around her, falling and dying on the sand because the others with them couldn't even pause to help without being cut down in turn. The only thing to do then was charge wildly, hoping that it would be enough.

They crashed in among the lines of defenses around the docks, and Kate leapt over a cannon, drawing her sword and cutting through the throat of one of the weapons crew. A man came at her with a bayonet, and Kate swayed aside from the attack, thrusting through his heart in response.

Around her, she could hear the clash of blades and the screams of dying men. The sounds of musket fire had slowed, at least, because this close in, there was no way for the Master of Crows' men to fire without hitting their own.

Men pressed in around Kate, but she didn't stop, fighting her way forward instead and cutting her way through the massed ranks of them. She parried a blow aimed at her stomach, then shoved aside a man who was targeting one of Lord Cranston's men with a pistol. A man swung an axe at her head and she ducked, stabbing upward into his abdomen.

Every step forward seemed to be slower now, as Kate found more and more enemies in her way. She tried to leap high over them, but their sheer numbers meant that she just came down in the middle of the fight again. She took a punch to the side of the head and retaliated with an elbow, then stepped away and stabbed.

There were too many opponents. She couldn't even use her powers to read the attacks coming in, and pressed in like this, even the mist that she'd managed to summon the last time she'd fought the New Army wouldn't make a difference. Their enemies already knew where Lord Cranston's men were.

More and more of them were dying. Kate saw men cut down around her, falling to bayonets and swords, axes and knives. She struck out at the enemy in front of her, but for every one she cut down, another was waiting to fill the gap. They formed a steadily contracting wall of flesh around her, moving closer in a ring of sharp edges.

Kate leapt again, up onto the shoulders of those who were attacking. She balanced on them the way she might have balanced when running from branch to branch in Siobhan's forest, stabbing down as she ran and leaping clear whenever an answering blade came up toward her. A shot whistled past her, but Kate kept moving. To stop now was to die.

She made for the ships, and managed to use the ropes tethering them to the docks as stepping stones, running across them, then heading up one onto the deck of a galleon. She grabbed a sealed lantern and lit it, even as a sailor ran at her. Kate smashed him out of the way with the lantern, feeling the crunch of it against his skull and hearing the glass sides shatter.

She threw it at the ship's sails and ran on as the flames licked at them.

With each ship she came to, Kate grabbed for another lantern, throwing it, moving as fast as she could. On the third, she saw a stock of black powder on the deck and aimed for that, sprinting from the boat as the flame she threw tumbled end over end toward it. The explosion behind her felt like being kicked in the back by a horse, even with the speed she was moving ahead of it.

Kate leapt for the deck of the next ship, her hands clinging onto the aft rail as she dragged herself aboard. A soldier ran at her with a blade and Kate slid past him on her knees, cutting him down as she passed.

Looking up, she saw a flag with a crow on it, feathers reaching out to touch all lands. It fluttered from the ship's mast like a taunt, or a threat. She had a moment to stare at it before another sailor was coming at her, Kate's blade having to flicker across to parry a curved saber. She sidestepped and cut back, then ran for the ship's mast.

She needed that flag. It was the closest thing to a standard that was there, and maybe, just maybe, once she had it they would be able to get out of there. Assuming that the others in Lord Cranston's company were still all right. For now, Kate had left them so far behind that she couldn't even see them. There were only enemies, which at least made things simpler when she knew that anyone coming toward her was doing it to try to kill her.

Kate climbed, starting out on the rigging of the ship. A sailor grabbed for her, and Kate kicked him away, seeing the man tumble down toward the water of the docks. She kept clambering upward until she reached the wide boom that held the lowest sail. She ran along it, then started to climb up the mast as if it were a tall tree.

She clung onto ropes until she reached the crows' nest above. There was a lookout there who stared at her, then grabbed for a knife. Kate reacted on instinct, shoving the man so that he fell end over end from the mast.

She reached up and cut down the flag, rolling it tightly and shoving it into her belt. She hoped that it would be enough. Now they could finally…

From her spot in the crows' nest, she could make out Lord Cranston, commanding his men far below. From the way he was limping, he'd been wounded, but he still fought, and still yelled commands as his men tried to hold off the soldiers in front of them.

Kate was more concerned about the second force that had come onto the approach to the city. Massed ranks of men marched toward Lord Cranston's men, effectively cutting them off from their escape route. To get clear, they would have to fight their way through the new enemy, but they couldn't hope to do that when they were already engaged with the foes in front of them.

Kate couldn't see a way for their forces to get past the new threat, and without that, there was only one outcome that she could see. They were going to die.

CHAPTER FIFTEEN

Sebastian pushed his fresh horse, and himself, as hard as he dared when he rode back to the crossroads. He'd ridden through the night, not caring about the risk of predators on the road of either the animal or the human kind, not caring about the risk of his horse missing its footing in the dark. By this point, he was so far behind Sophia that he needed to make up any ground he could.

Would she be happy to see him when he caught up to her? The fact that she'd sent him the wrong way suggested that she wasn't pleased at the prospect, but Sebastian would make her see that he was a different man from the one who had pushed her aside for fear of what his family would say. He would show her that he loved her, and that she had nothing to fear from him.

If this were some minstrel's song, of course, he would already have found her. In those, gallant knights from the days when there had been such things had ridden after their lady loves and found them quickly, after only a series of trials to test their resolve. They had declared their love, and that had been more than enough.

They hadn't typically gotten lost.

That Sebastian had been misled didn't matter. What mattered was that he was further away from Sophia than ever, having to ride hard just to make up the time he'd lost in his pursuit of her. When he finally made it back to the crossroads, he breathed a sigh of relief, but the truth was that he still had a long way to go.

He didn't even know how far. Sophia was heading north, but where was she going?

The drunk who had been by the crossroads wasn't there now. Sebastian was grateful for that in a way, because he wasn't sure how he would have reacted to the man who had tried to keep him from Sophia, if he had been there. Sebastian turned his horse northward, and he heeled it forward even though both he and the beast were starting to tire.

Eventually, though, he had to stop at an inn, if only to change horses. He asked after Sophia when he stopped, of course. To his surprise, the landlord there remembered her.

"Aye, she came past. Sold me some very strange-tasting beer and asked after the way to Monthys."

"Monthys?" Sebastian said. "You're sure?"

The landlord shrugged. "I think so."

"And she didn't pay you to say that to anyone who asked? This isn't some kind of trick?"

The other man frowned at him. "Why would someone do that?"

Sebastian didn't bother trying to explain it. Instead, he kept riding north, taking a fresh horse because he didn't want to risk killing his mount with the speed he was asking it to travel for so many hours. He thundered along roads that were paved only in places, having to slow on the sections that were little more than dirt, then trying to make up time on the better section. Whenever he passed travelers, Sebastian stopped to ask them if they had seen Sophia. Most hadn't, but the few who did remember passing her on the road said the same as the innkeeper had: she was heading for Monthys.

Sebastian tried to work out what she could want in Monthys. The only thing he knew was there was the ruined home of the former noble family the Danses, who were all long dead. Was she heading for that? If so, what did Sophia hope to find? It made no sense to Sebastian, but even so, it gave him something to aim for.

As Sebastian rode north, the weather started to worsen. He could feel the temperature dropping around him, so that he had to wrap his cloak tighter and tighter around himself to keep the cold out. At least that meant that when the rain hit, it was already in place to keep some of it off. Not much, but some.

The rain seemed constant. It started as a chilly drizzle that seemed almost to hang in the air, waiting for Sebastian to ride through it. Then it became something heavier, until he might have been riding through a stream given how wet it was. Lightning flashed in the distance, and Sebastian knew that the safe thing to do would be to stop with his horse until the worst of the weather passed.

He didn't, though. He had to catch up to Sophia.

Lightning flickered down again, and now it struck a tree by the road, wood flying as its sap boiled. The tree flared in flames, despite the rain, and Sebastian's horse reared. It was all he could do to cling to it as it bucked in terror. It set off at a full gallop away from the sound, and Sebastian clung to it, knowing that there was no chance of bringing it under control when it was so frightened.

All he could do was let it run, trying to soothe it until finally the maddened creature's bolt for freedom turned into a run, then a walk. Eventually, Sebastian managed to bring it under control. He dismounted, walking the horse for a while as the rain slackened, but then rode on again.

He came to a river and rode downstream until he found a place to cross, then eventually came to another inn, where the locals stared at him as if expecting him to attack them at any moment. When he mentioned Sophia, their expressions only darkened further.

"Seems there's a lot of people asking that," the landlord said. "Are you going to rent a room?"

Sebastian did so, although he had no intention of stopping there. In return, he got a bowl of soup that tasted mostly of turnips and onions, a mug of ale, and the news that Sophia had been through, still heading north to Monthys, accompanied by the two other women he'd heard about, and a forest cat, which he hadn't.

He set off again as quickly as he dared, pushing his horse through the landscape of rocks, moss, heather, and scrubby grass. There were sheep there as well as goats, clinging precariously to the side of hills that seemed impossible to farm but that held fields nevertheless. Trees clung to them, windblown and stretched by the extremes of the climate.

Sebastian plowed on through it, but he slowed when he saw the bodies ahead. There were two of them, lying on flat stones near the road, apparently left where they'd fallen. As Sebastian got closer, he saw that they were a man and a woman, both dressed in a way that Sebastian associated with the rough people of the road.

"Highwaymen," Sebastian said.

Dead highwaymen, with only a few signs of what had happened to them. The man had a stab wound that suggested how he'd died, but the woman had no obvious marks on her beyond a faint discoloration to her features that might have spoken of either poison or strangulation. There were signs that they had been robbed of whatever weapons they'd had, suggesting to Sebastian that maybe they'd run into a more dangerous opponent on the road.

Had they attacked Sophia? That thought quashed whatever pity Sebastian might have felt for them. Certainly, these people would have tried to attack *someone*, and if it was Sophia, then he was glad they had failed.

And failed recently. That thought came to him as he stared at them. No animals had been there to chew at their dead flesh yet. The rain and the ravages of time hadn't started to decompose their corpses. That meant that whoever had passed must have done so within the last day or so, maybe even the last few hours. Sebastian hurried back to his horse.

Under other circumstances, he might have stopped to bury the dead robbers, but now there was no time to lose. He all but leapt onto his horse and rode on.

How far had he ridden now? It was hard to say precisely, because Sebastian wasn't sure exactly where he was. Even if he had known, the maps of the kingdom were often things put together with more guesswork than precision, individual nobles paying for maps of their holdings, or cities seeking plans of the surrounding areas. If there had ever been a systematic attempt to map the kingdom, it had gone with the civil wars.

All Sebastian knew was that he hadn't ridden far enough yet, because he still hadn't caught up to Sophia. He pressed on through the hills, staring ahead as if he could will her to be around the next bend in the track. There were fewer people here than almost anywhere else he'd been, but whenever Sebastian saw one of the rare shepherds there, he called out to them, hoping they'd seen her.

He was tired now; bone tired with the feeling that he might fall from his horse if he didn't reach his destination soon. It felt as though he had been riding forever, and even the bowl of soup at the inn seemed like a lifetime ago.

Sebastian was so tired that when he heard the rumble of the rocks, he almost didn't recognize it for what it was. It wasn't until he saw the rocks tumbling toward him down one of the hillsides that he recognized the landslide for what it was. The rains must have loosened rocks above, washing away the soil that held them in place. Now, they came down at him.

He pulled his horse to one side, heeling it forward as boulders rolled past, trying to get up onto the far slope, where he might be safe. Sebastian forced his horse forward, knowing that if just one of those rocks hit its legs, it would fall, and he would go down with it. Even if the next rocks didn't finish him, he would still be stuck miles from anywhere, forced to walk after Sophia far slower than her cart could take her away from him.

A low stone wall marked the boundary of the pathway. He urged his horse into a leap and felt its muscles bunch as it gathered itself to jump. It leapt, and Sebastian felt the moment when its hooves brushed the top of the wall, but it didn't falter. It sprang forward, up the hill, and Sebastian turned it back to where the rocks were still rumbling forward. They crashed against the wall, almost flattening it before coming to a halt at the base of the hill.

Sebastian was starting to feel as if even the landscape was trying to keep him from Sophia. He dismounted, leading his horse back down to the path as carefully as he could, picking his way through the field of boulders that now all but covered the path. Right then, he felt as though he barely had the strength to remount. Only the thought of Sophia at the end of this search gave him the strength to do it.

His horse plodded forward now on exhausted legs. Sebastian could understand it, and if he had been doing anything else, he would have let the horse rest. When it came to Sophia, though, he pushed forward, along the pathways leading to Monthys. He rode up the next hill, struggling his way to the top.

As he reached the crest, he saw the bridge in the distance, its white marble shining dully, the gaps in its structure looking like wounds filled in by moss and vines. Beyond it, Sebastian could see the hills and woods of Monthys, seeming almost like a prelude to the mountain lands beyond them. Sebastian hoped he wouldn't have to go that far. The people he'd passed had seemed clear that this was where Sophia was heading.

More than that, he could see hints of her destination there beyond the hills, in the crenulations and stonework of a house that must have been standing there as long as the hills. It had to be the Danses' old estate that Sophia was heading for, even if Sebastian couldn't imagine why she would do so. He didn't even think that there would be anyone living there after all this time.

The reason didn't matter though. What mattered was that Sophia would be there. He was closer to her now than he had been in days, and soon he would be with her, holding her in his arms. Compared with that prospect, nothing else mattered.

Sebastian rode down toward the bridge with hope in his heart once more.

CHAPTER SIXTEEN

Sophia stared at the crossbow leveled at her, knowing that there would be no way to dive aside in time if the man there pulled the trigger. Beside her, she felt Sienne tense, obviously getting ready to leap, and she could sense from the new figure's mind that he would fire as soon as the forest cat moved.

"Just stay calm," she said, to both Sienne and the man with the crossbow. "We aren't here to cause any trouble."

"Wait," the man said. "I know that voice. I know that face. But it can't be. Who *are* you?"

"My name is Sophia," Sophia said.

"By the gods, it *is* you," the man said. He lowered his crossbow. "I took you for Lady Christina for a moment, but no, I recognize you now. You're her daughter. Do you remember me?"

He stepped forward where Sophia could see him. He was wild-haired, with the tangled beard of a man who probably didn't see others much. Despite that, he wore the colors of a noble family's retainer, green and black well faded by time. Sophia thought she was going to have to tell him that she didn't know him, or pluck his name from his mind to pretend, but to her surprise, her memory supplied a name.

"It's McCallum, isn't it?" she said. "You... you used to get me and Kate to help you prune the roses. Kate used to love hacking things down."

She had a memory of her sister, tiny and fierce, attacking a plant with pruning shears as if it were an enemy to be defeated, while this man, the head gardener, had tried to contain the chaos.

"She did," McCallum said with a smile. "Made my job twice as hard."

He put the crossbow down now, moving forward. Sienne growled, obviously thinking that there was still a threat, and Sophia calmed her, moving forward to hug the gardener.

"What are you doing here?" Sophia asked, looking around at the house, so empty except for him. "Where *is* everybody?"

McCallum shook his head. "It's just me. It has been ever since everything that happened. I keep out the animals and the folk who think that they can just come in to loot. It's what I took you for until I saw who you were. Your friends aren't looters, are they?"

Sophia had the sense of a man who had been there alone for far too long, so that he'd lost connection with reality at least a little. Sophia did her best to tether him to it.

"No, they're not," she said. "This is Emeline, and this is Cora. They're my friends. And this is Sienne," she added, gesturing to the forest cat. "I know it might not look like it, but she's friendly, too."

"If you say so, miss," the former gardener said. "Would you like to come somewhere comfortable and have a bite to eat?"

"I'd like that," Sophia said with a smile, even though right then the only thing she wanted to do was bombard the man with questions.

Emeline didn't look convinced by it. "I doubt there's any food here that isn't rotten."

"Oh no, not here," McCallum said. "Follow me."

Sophia thought about telling him that she wasn't done looking around, but the truth was that, however many memories the house held for her, the gardener had the potential for real answers. So she followed, down through the house on a route she remembered running down with her sister whenever their nurse had told them they could play in the gardens. She followed McCallum, and the others followed her, obviously trusting that she knew what she was doing. She didn't; she was just hoping that there would be more answers waiting for her.

They walked out through the back of the house, on the side that couldn't be seen so easily from the road. There was a square of garden there that was far neater than the overgrown mess of the rest of it, with a small cottage at its heart that Sophia remembered from her childhood. It had a thatched roof and white painted walls, carefully maintained.

"I tried to do the best I could with the grounds," McCallum said, as he showed them to the cottage, "but the truth is that it's too much for one man, and when I did... well, it made some folk think that it was a good place for them to come."

The cottage wasn't like the house. The house had been a dust-filled mausoleum, perfectly preserved in a moment in time. This was a living home, with all the mess and clutter that entailed. There was a cauldron bubbling with porridge over a low fire, and a rough wooden table at the heart of the room. Sophia and the others went to it while the gardener set out bowls of the porridge for them. Cora and Emeline took theirs gratefully.

Then there were the ravens.

91

They cawed and looked down from every rafter and cranny. There were the remnants of cages here and there in the cottage's main room, but none of the ravens were in them.

"His Lordship's old messenger birds," McCallum explained. "I couldn't just leave them in the house. The poor things would have starved. Besides… I like the company."

As Sophia watched, one hopped down to the gardener, and he fed it a scrap of meat.

"Can you tell me about what happened?" Sophia asked.

"But you were there," McCallum pointed out.

She shook her head. "I remember… some of it. Snatches. I was too young to remember all of it, and I don't think I ever knew how it all fit together. I need to know… do you know what happened to my parents?"

She scanned his thoughts for any clue, unwilling to leave this to chance. Even so, when the gardener spoke next, she knew that he was telling the truth.

"I wish I could help you," McCallum said. Sophia could feel the sadness coming off him then like mist from a lake. "I never saw them after the night when the killers came. I never saw any of you. Some of the others told me that you'd obviously all been killed in the chaos, but here *you* are, so I was right to hold out hope! I was right!"

Again, Sophia had the sense of a man who'd been alone for so long and suffered so much that he only had a tenuous grip on the world around him. She could see Cora looking at him with pity, Emeline with a faint roll of her eyes. Sophia decided to try a slightly different tack.

"Can you tell me about what happened that night?" she asked.

McCallum went still, then finally nodded. "All right. You deserve that much at least. I remember the rumors among the staff leading up to it. Some of us had been saying that there would be trouble, that the Dowager wouldn't just let things go, not after her husband died in the war, but the others told us that we were being stupid and all anyone wanted was peace. They just saw what they wanted to see."

Sophia could understand that. She could imagine people grabbing for any chance at peace after a long war. She remembered what her mother had written: that her family had accepted being no more than nobles just so the first round of wars would stop. Wasn't this just the same thing?

"People don't pay attention," Emeline said, still eating her porridge. A raven landed near her and she shooed it away.

"They came for us, and it was too late," McCallum said. "So many people died that night. Not just in this house, either. I've heard stories of nobles as far away as Charlke dying because they were big supporters of your family, or they had magic, or both."

"That sounds awful," Cora said.

Sophia could imagine that kind of violence sweeping the kingdom all too easily. The peace might have been agreed, but one single night of murder had flickered across it all like wildfire, ensuring that the Dowager would at least have the better of what came next.

"When it was done, there was no one left to protect the lands around here," McCallum said. "There's still the fishing port to the east, but mostly, people left the lands here to the robbers once your parents' protection was gone."

"How many people died?" Sophia asked.

McCallum shook his head. "In the kingdom? I don't know. Hundreds at least, maybe more. Here?" His voice turned stony. "I had to bury twenty-seven once it was done, out on the edges of the grounds. They killed whoever they could get hold of. Servant, soldier, family, it didn't matter to them. I only survived because..."

He trailed off, but Sophia could see the truth of it written in his thoughts. He'd been out in the grounds working when the violence had come, and when he'd seen it, he'd stood there, knowing he should help, but unable to bring himself to move.

"It's all right," Sophia said, reaching across the table to take his hand. "If you'd gone inside, they'd have killed you too."

She heard him choke back a sob. Now even Emeline looked at him with pity.

"I'd forgotten what you can do," he said. "You and your sister used to make me play guessing games even though we all knew that you'd see whatever I guessed."

"You don't have to feel guilty," Sophia said. "Staying here like this, you've done more than anyone could have asked of you."

"You... you don't know how much it means to hear that from you," McCallum said. "It's a fine thing to do, assuaging an old man's guilt like that. You'd make a fine lady of the house."

"That's a kind thing for you to say," Sophia said.

The gardener stood, gesturing out the window of his cottage toward the main body of the house. "No, I mean it, my lady. Why not stay? You could have the house, it's still livable enough, and I could work on the gardens, and I'm sure you could attract some servants once they knew that you were back."

In its way, it was actually tempting. Sophia could imagine herself in this house. She could send for her sister and...

...and things still wouldn't be the way they had been before. That was gone. She'd come here looking for her parents, and all that she'd found of them here was a letter, pointing to her uncle, Lars Skyddar. Between her and the gardener, it seemed that everyone had an idea about what she should do next. Everyone had a dream for her, whether it was her parents' dream of her taking the throne, the gardener's dream of rebuilding, or Kate's old hope that they would both travel the world together while Kate fought. Even Cora and Emeline had their dream of finding Stonehome, with its safety for people like them.

What was Sophia's dream? What did she want? The answer to that was simple enough: she wanted to find her parents.

"I'm sorry," she said, "but I can't stay."

The gardener frowned at that. "But miss, this is your home."

Sophia shook her head. "It *was* my home," she said, "and maybe it will be again one day, but home for me means family, and I still haven't found mine."

She saw the other girls frown at that.

"The idea was that we would come here, and then go on to Stonehome," Emeline pointed out.

Cora nodded. "I thought we were going somewhere safe, not going on traveling."

Sophia could understand that. Even so, this was what she wanted. Not all of what she wanted, though.

"Mr. McCallum, do you think any of your ravens would remember the way to the palace?" she asked.

"You want to start sending the Dowager messages?" Emeline asked.

You know it's for Sebastian, Sophia sent over to her.

"I think so," McCallum said. "Ravens are clever birds. They remember."

Sophia nodded at that. "Cora, can you go back into the house and fetch me writing paper and ink, please?"

Cora at least didn't argue about it, just went to fetch what was needed. McCallum and Emeline were still looking at her expectantly, as if she might have changed her mind about one of their plans for her.

"I'm not staying to run the house," Sophia said, "and I'm not going to Stonehome. My plan is to go and find my uncle. My parents' plan to use him to take back the kingdom is... well, I don't want that, but maybe he'll at least know where they are and how I can get to them."

"And the raven for Sebastian?" Emeline asked.

That was one thing Sophia felt as though she had to do.

"Sebastian is the father of my child," she said. "He at least deserves to know that he is going to become a parent. He needs to have a chance to follow."

"And what *else* are you going to tell him?" Emeline asked. "Are you going to tell him that you're good enough for his mother's standards now?"

Sophia could hear the note of bitterness there.

You think I'm abandoning you because I don't need you, don't you? she sent across to Emeline.

Isn't that what you're doing? You're a noble.

Sophia shook her head. "I'm not going to tell Sebastian who I really am. The news of his child should be enough. If he'll come to me when he hears that, then I know he's everything I hoped he was. If it takes the knowledge of who I am, then I'm not sure that I would want to be with him after all."

Put like that, the future seemed simple. She would send her raven, head for her uncle's house across the sea, and hope that it would be enough to bring Sebastian following on behind her. If he did that, it would prove how he felt. If he didn't… well, that would prove something too.

CHAPTER SEVENTEEN

Angelica could see the great house away in the distance, its dilapidation an affront to her sensibilities. A noble should maintain their home, if only to declare to those around them that they were fulfilling their natural role in the world. Letting a grand house fall into disrepair was a declaration of ordinariness, of lost status, of *weakness*.

Then again, this wasn't a living house, but a corpse, meant to be a statement as surely as one left in a gibbet might be. The statement was simple: those who crossed the Dowager suffered for it, whatever the law said about royal power being curtailed. It was one more reason why Angelica didn't intend to fail in her task.

Her task? Call it what it was. She had to murder Sophia.

Angelica was a touch surprised by how little it bothered her. Killing the bandits before had been nothing, and she supposed that she had destroyed enough lives before now even if she hadn't actually taken them with her own hands. There was a kind of power to it that Angelica liked. Being able to determine if someone succeeded or failed at court was one thing, but being able to decide if they lived or died was more direct, and more powerful.

"Be careful," she told herself as she rode closer to the house. She doubted there would be any friends to her within it, and she had no way of knowing how many others besides Sophia were there. At the very least, the rumors on the road said that she had two human companions and some kind of dangerous pet. Riding up to the house, seen long before she got there over the open lawns, would be suicide.

So Angelica waited on the rise before the house, staring down at it as she tried to plan her next move. If she could work out where Sophia would be, she could plan a suitable ambush. The trick was guessing where she would go next. Guess wrong, and she would lose her prey as surely as Sebastian had when Angelica had sent him to Barriston.

She was still considering the problem when she saw the raven rise from the house.

It flew up from it, no more than a dark speck at first, drifting up into the blue of the sky in a flurry of wings. As messenger birds, they were common enough. Angelica recognized it for what it was almost instantly. The question was what she wanted to do about it, because there could be only one reason that the creature was coming from an empty house like that.

Angelica's fingers brushed the pistols that she'd taken from the bandits. It was a stupid thought. Short-barreled flintlocks like these could kill a man at close range, but with their smooth barrels, they were as likely to miss as hit anything more than a dozen yards away. The odds of hitting a bird in flight at this kind of distance were far too remote.

What she needed in this situation was a bow, or a hunting falcon, although even there, propriety demanded that a noblewoman of her station stuck to the smallest and most delicate of hawks. People used ravens rather than doves exactly because they were harder to bring down.

Angelica's fists whitened in anger at not being able to do anything about the bird. She didn't know what its message would say, but it would be too much of a coincidence if it said nothing about Sophia. Worse, the fact that it was flying at all said that she'd been right to avoid the house. There were other people in there besides Sophia, or there would have been no stock of ravens to send.

Angelica was still fuming when she saw the raven change direction, heading straight toward her. The incongruity of it all made her laugh. Was the bird so stupid that it had decided to simply fly to the first person it saw? It was too much to hope for, yet it seemed to be happening.

The raven hung above her in the air, circling as it flew lower. Angelica couldn't make sense of it. Trained birds just didn't do this. They flew to the places they were trained to fly. It didn't even make sense to say that maybe the creature had become confused about where it was, or had lost its instinct for its task, because then it would simply have flown off into the surrounding countryside.

Instead, it circled lower until it landed on a stone not far from her. It was a large thing, probably big enough that Angelica would have struggled to perch it on her arm. It regarded her with deep black eyes that showed no hint of emotion, staring at her from one side and then the other in the way birds did to get a sense of something that wasn't moving.

"A gift," it cawed, and Angelica almost fell from her horse in shock. She'd known that corvids could be trained to talk—Lady

Harriston of the Netherfields insisted on keeping mynah birds that blurted out the most inappropriate things—but she'd never heard of a messenger bird doing it.

"A gift," it repeated, "from the Master of Crows."

Angelica had heard that name as a rumor. They said that he could see through the eyes of his crows, watching advancing armies from above while the beasts circled, waiting for the carrion of battle. She'd assumed that it was a joke, or a way of turning a perfectly ordinary general into some kind of demon to be defeated at all costs. Now, she wasn't so sure.

The raven kept blinking at her, hopping from side to side as it waited. Carefully, Angelica pulled one of the pistols from her belt, testing the weight of it. Something seemed to change in that instant, like the flicker of someone moving from sleep to wakefulness. The bird froze in place for a moment, then flexed its wings. It fluttered them, and in another second it was airborne again.

On instinct, Angelica lifted the pistol, not caring whether anyone heard her now. She was closer, and at this range, she at least had a chance. She fired, the sound of the shot enough to make her horse rear so that she had to cling to it just to avoid falling. The acrid smoke from the thing filled the air around her, stinging Angelica's eyes as she struggled to keep her seat in the saddle. It was the better part of a minute before her horse calmed enough that she felt safe to dismount, holding the reins firmly so that it wouldn't run.

The raven lay dead on the ground a little way away, reduced to little more than blood and feathers by the impact of her shot. Angelica knelt beside it, and while she hadn't felt anything at the deaths of the bandits who had attacked her, she could feel herself shaking now.

It wasn't the violence. Angelica didn't care about violence, although she typically found herself approaching it with the distaste of someone who could afford to have others do it for her. She *did* care about the strangeness of what had just happened. She might only spend the bare minimum of time in the Masked Goddess's temples, but she knew about the abominations of magic, and this was definitely one.

The thought of it made her shudder, although probably not for the reasons the priests would have wished. They might hate magic because it was a power that didn't come from their goddess; Angelica's reaction had more to do with power that she couldn't control or influence, that didn't care what connections she had or what wealth her family had accumulated.

She didn't like the sense of being caught up in something bigger than herself. It was bad enough being the pawn of the Dowager in this, without the sense that some strange power was taking an interest in her affairs.

Even so, she made her way over to the remains of the raven, picking the tightly rolled message from the still stick of its leg. She waited until her fingers stopped shaking before she unrolled it. Once she'd spread out the small scrap of parchment, she started to read.

My dearest Sebastian, she read, and had to fight the urge to tear it up there and then, simply because of the claim it made on the man who should be her husband by now. Instead, she read on.

If you are reading this, know that I am safe, and that I love you. There are things that I must tell you, and no easy way to say them. I hope to be able to say most of them to you in person, if you follow.

For now, though, there is one thing that you must know: I am with child. Your child.

Angelica snorted at that. It was the same claim that any milkmaid might make when trying to trap one of her betters. It was a ploy as old as time, and it almost didn't matter that it might prove to be true, or that Angelica had been planning something very similar when it came to Sebastian. What mattered was that Sophia was making a move in a game she probably didn't even know she was playing. Well, it was a move that Angelica could counter. *Had* countered, the moment she shot this beast.

She kept reading anyway, because she wanted to be thorough.

I hope that news fills you with happiness, not hurt or fear. I know that it is news that would be better to hear face to face, but you deserve to know about your child even if you do not choose to follow. It is something that I dreamed of when we were together, and I have dreamed since. I believe our child will be something special, and will make you proud.

Angelica felt that Sophia was trying too hard there. It would have been better just to hint and leave it at that. All this nonsense about dreams just made her sound delusional, and Angelica doubted that even Sebastian would find that a desirable quality in a woman.

I hope that you will follow me. I want to be with you, and I hope that you want to be with me too, in spite of everything that has happened. I love you. I don't ever want to be apart from you again. If you are going to follow me, you will find me in Ishjemme, in the court of Lars Skyddar. I'm told that there are docks to the east of Monthys, and I will head there soon to try to find a ship. I truly hope that you will come there, or follow me to Ishjemme, because it

99

aches to be without you. I miss you more than anything, and I have a lot of things to tell you.

Angelica didn't know what those things were, or even if they existed at all. If she were the one sending the letter, that was what she might have done: hint at things enough that even if Sebastian were undecided, he would make the journey just to find out the rest, then trust that once they were close, she could find a way to persuade him.

Was Sophia trying the same thing? She'd been cunning enough to pretend to be someone she wasn't, so Angelica didn't discount the possibility. Even so, there was a note here that made it sound as though these really were the desperate words of a jilted lover. Then again, maybe Sophia was simply that good at pretending.

"It doesn't matter," Angelica said. "This will be done soon."

What did she feel at the prospect that Sophia was pregnant? Angelica cocked her head to one side as she examined that question. Anger, of course, at the prospect of it being true. Some contempt at the possibility it might simply be a manipulation. Was there any sympathy? Anything that might stop her from killing Sophia while she held Sebastian's child inside her?

Angelica was a little surprised to find that she felt nothing at the prospect. Not sympathy, not disgust, not anger, just… nothing. It didn't make a difference to her, except maybe in that it made the whole thing even more necessary. Sebastian was the kind of man who might find himself tied to a girl like this by some sense of duty.

He was also the kind of man who wouldn't forgive himself if he learned of the death of his child. It would break something in him, and Angelica had no wish to have that happen. She wanted Sebastian as he was, vibrant and strong enough that they could have real power after their marriage.

That meant that he could never know about this. *Any* of this. He couldn't know that Angelica was there. He couldn't know that Sophia was going across the sea. He *definitely* couldn't know about the possibility of her being pregnant. No, he needed to be kept safely in the dark, wandering around in Barriston, while Angelica dealt with the situation.

Very carefully, she tore the parchment into strips, then poured out a measure of black powder onto it, using the flint from one of the pistols against the metal of its barrel to provide a spark. It flared and caught, quickly consumed by the flames that licked at it.

If only Sophia were so easy to be rid of. Still, at least Angelica knew where she was going to be now, and a busy set of docks was a much easier place in which to get close to someone than an empty country estate. Angelica would kill her, no one would know how it had happened, and finally, *finally,* this would be over.

CHAPTER EIGHTEEN

From her perch atop the ship, Kate saw the advance of the New Army along the beach and knew that there would be no way to break through them to escape now. Lord Cranston's men were trapped as surely as a poacher in steel jaws, unable to press forward or back, caught between two forces that could easily crush them.

And the worst part was that it was her fault. If she hadn't killed the people she had, if Lord Cranston hadn't taken her in when the church of the Masked Goddess wanted her dead, his company would probably never have been sent here. She had to fix this. She *had* to.

Could she summon mist, as she had on the shores near Ashton? Kate reached for that fragment of power, but the truth was that she had no idea how to use it consciously. Worse, things felt... different somehow here, as if that power were a distant thing, waiting for her at home. She could still feel the minds of those on the beach, but she wasn't sure that she could do more than that.

"I have to," Kate told herself. At the very least, she had to do *something*. So she tied the flag she'd seized around herself, checked that her sword was secure in its scabbard, and leapt.

She cut through the air, arcing clear of the ship as she dove, her arms extending above her head to break the impact of the water. Kate plunged into it, feeling the shock of the cold there, and the weight of the water as it dragged at her clothes, threatening to pull her down. She was just grateful that her mobile style of fighting meant she avoided heavy armor.

Kate hauled herself to the surface, then set off in strong strokes toward the shore. Behind her, Kate could see ships burning as the fires she'd set caught. It wasn't many of the enemy ships, but it was something, at least. One was already burning from top to bottom, its sails seemingly made from the fire that consumed them as men threw themselves from the deck in an effort to find safety.

The current wouldn't let her come out exactly where Lord Cranston's men were. Instead, she found herself just a little way behind them, closer to the new group of attackers than to her own side. Kate drew herself up to her full height as the advancing group stared at her, obviously trying to decide which of them would kill her.

"I have their flag!" Kate yelled back to where Lord Cranston's men were still fighting. "We can pull back!"

She saw the men fighting there, swords flashing, daggers and axes working in short arcs. The time for muskets was long done; now there was just the bloody, close in work of the melee, and the press of bodies on all sides, for them. She saw Lord Cranston, limping from a wound, slice a cut across a man's throat, then gesture in her direction.

"Pull back!" he ordered, his voice carrying even above the screams and the sound of steel on steel. "Fight your way through!"

They came, but in that moment, Kate had other concerns. The enemies closer to her were leveling their weapons now, obviously getting ready for a devastating volley of musket fire. Kate thought about throwing herself flat, but that wouldn't do anything to save the others, and in any case, she would be left at their mercy when they charged. She had to do something else.

So she did.

Kate had managed mind control with small groups back in Siobhan's forest, but she had never tried it with so many people, or with so much at stake. Now, though, she knew that she had to try, because if she didn't, they were all dead. She reached out, feeling for the minds of the enemy soldiers, identifying them and entering into them.

Then she clamped down like a torturer's vise around a hand, pinning them in place, allowing no movement, allowing no thought.

The effort of it was immense. It felt like trying to crush the life from a bear while it fought, and for a moment, Kate simply wasn't sure that she would have the strength. She could feel the wetness of blood on her lip as her nose bled with the strain of it, her head feeling as though it might explode with the effort of what she was trying to do. She held out a hand, willing her power to be enough.

The advancing company of the New Army's men froze in place like statues, their weapons still raised to fire. Kate knew that they *weren't* statues, though. They were simply men who couldn't summon enough thoughts to make even the small decision to pull a trigger. She held them like that, smothering their thoughts, holding them in place, while around her, Lord Cranston's men surged past.

They slammed into the immobile soldiers like a scythe, cutting men down left and right, punching a path through them that they could follow. Kate ran after them, and even that was enough that she lost a few of the men she was holding, but she kept her grip on the others even while the clash of blades sounded ahead.

She plunged into the fight, her blade cutting down men as they struggled to rouse themselves. She hacked and moved, never staying in one place, killing with all the speed and power of a cannonball plunging through them. She had to buy the others time to break through and make it to the ships. She owed them that when they wouldn't even have been there if it weren't for her.

Then she felt the other force pushing at the edges of her power, breaking it apart and scattering it. It felt like some great, fluttering thing, dark and dangerous, too strong to hold against here, like this. Kate felt her hold on the soldiers give way in a collapse of fragments, unable to hold them. Around her, she heard the blare of muskets as men did what they'd been intending when she'd gripped their minds, but Lord Cranston's men were already past.

They came at her now, and Kate had to move and dodge, feeling the whisper of blades too close to her, cutting back with her own weapons at throat and groin, heart and shoulder. She was red with blood now, so that the rest of her must have matched her hair, leaving her looking like some kind of creature out of nightmares.

Then Kate saw someone who was.

He appeared to be no more than twenty or so, yet there was something ageless about his face as he stalked through the battle. He had dark hair that was spiked and flicked until it seemed like the unruly feathers of a bird. His eyes were covered by dark glasses that made it seem as though his eyes had no whites to them. He wore the ochre of the others, but over it, there was a long coat of dark material, scuffed and marked by years of use. His gloved hands gripped the hilt of a long dueling sword, which cut out with deadly grace whenever someone got too close. As if to declare who he was, a crow rode on his shoulder, black eyes staring.

The Master of Crows came forward, and Kate knew that he was coming for her.

She leapt to meet him, her own sword flashing up to strike toward his throat. He parried the blow and slipped aside, his riposte coming so fast that Kate barely avoided it.

"You have some skill," he said, parrying another attack. "And you have some power. Would you like to know what I do with those who have power?"

"Talk them to death?" Kate guessed, throwing another attack halfway through it. The Master of Crows was fast enough to whirl away.

"I put what's left of them in cages for the crows to feast on and take their power," the Master of Crows replied. "I'm sure my pets will enjoy devouring you. First, though, we need to make you carrion."

He struck at Kate then, and he was brutally fast. His first cut almost broke through her defenses. His second did, and Kate felt a flash of pain as his sword struck into the meat of her arm. Kate barely managed to kick him away, making space.

She knew in that moment that she couldn't beat him. Not here, not like this. She threw another cut anyway, and the Master of Crows deflected it with a circling parry that almost drew Kate onto the tip of his blade.

"Kate! Get down!"

Kate heard the urgency in Lord Cranston's tone and dropped to the ground without hesitation. Behind her, she heard the roar of muskets, and she saw men fall, but the Master of Crows was lost amid the smoke and the sounds of the battle.

A part of Kate thought about going after him, but that would be suicide. Instead, she forced herself to her feet, running back toward Lord Cranston's forces. They ran together, Kate helping to support the older man as they made their way back to the boats. They clambered aboard, scrambling up netting while above them, sailors were already working to put the ships into motion. Kate all but fell onto the deck, lying there while around her, men struggled aboard. She didn't know how many there were now, because there was no way of knowing how many might have been cut down in the battle.

She felt the ship swinging round, heading out to sea, and Kate made herself stand. To her surprise, none of the vessels in the harbor seemed to be following them now. Perhaps they didn't believe that they were worth the effort. As if in answer to that thought, words whispered in her mind, in a brush that made her shudder.

Don't worry, girl, I will come for you soon. You, your mistress, and all the old things of the world.

Kate had no doubt that he meant it.

***

As the ship sailed the distance back across the Knifewater, Kate looked around at the men who sat nursing wounds or washing blood away from their armor. She walked the length of the ship, looking for Will, and as she did so, she caught the thoughts around her.

105

It's her fault so many are dead.
It's her fault we were there.
It's her fault...

Kate clamped down on her powers simply to stop hearing it, but that didn't do anything to get rid of the hard looks as she passed or the muttering behind her back. After the first battle she'd been in, Kate had found herself feeling that she was finally starting to fit in with the company. Now, she felt as though she would never truly be one of them.

She found Will in the space near the cannons, packing away unused powder. To Kate's shock, he had a bandage wrapped around his arm, through which blood was seeping.

"Will? What happened?" she demanded.

She'd hoped he would be safe back on the ship, firing cannon in support of the assault. She'd been sure that he had one of the safest roles in Lord Cranston's company.

"One of the cannon kicked back," Will said. "It could have happened at any time."

"At any time in a battle," Kate said. "And that battle wouldn't have happened if it weren't for me."

"You mustn't think like that," Will insisted. He reached out for her, but Kate stepped back.

"What else am I supposed to think?" Kate demanded. She shook her head as Will moved forward again. "I have to go. I have to... Lord Cranston will be asking for me by now."

She hurried off, and in the confined space of the ship, it didn't take long to find the company's commander. He was in his cabin, pouring alcohol over a wound that looked as though it had come from a dagger.

"What is it, Kate?" he asked. "I have rather a lot to do."

Kate took a breath, then said it before she could talk herself out of it. "I think I need to leave your company, sir."

Lord Cranston regarded her for several seconds. "Why do you say that?"

"You know why," Kate said. "As long as I'm a part of your company, you're all in danger. The Dowager will continue to send you on suicide missions. This should have killed us all, and it wouldn't have happened if it weren't for me."

"We wouldn't have *survived* if it weren't for you," Lord Cranston pointed out. He stopped pouring the alcohol on his wounds and took a swig of it instead. "You fired their ships. You took their flag."

"None of which would have been necessary if it weren't for my presence," Kate said. "You need to let me go. Drop me off somewhere on the coast and just go."

Lord Cranston paused with his flask halfway to his lips. "You realize what you're suggesting, Kate? You wouldn't have the protection of the company anymore. You would go back to being hunted. You wouldn't be safe."

"I'm not safe anyway," Kate said. "At least, this way, all of you might be."

Lord Cranston stood, moving over to the window to his cabin.

"No. No, Kate, I won't allow it."

"You have to," Kate insisted.

He spun back toward her. "I don't *have* to do any such thing. You'll die out there if you go off alone, and I'll not let that happen."

Kate shook her head, ready to argue, but Lord Cranston cut her off.

"I have asked your opinion on many things, Kate, but this is one matter that is not up for discussion. I am the commander of this company, and I have made my decision. You will stay with us, where you can be safe. If that attracts the Dowager's wrath then... well, we will find a way to deal with it."

Kate knew he was trying to protect her, but even so, it was a stupid move.

"You know that this won't keep anyone safe?" she said.

"If need be, I'll lock you in the hold for your own protection," Lord Cranston said. "Do I need to do that?"

He sounded as though he was serious, and Kate had seen how implacable he could be before.

Kate shook her head. "No, sir."

"Good," Lord Cranston said with a smile. "We'll find a way to get through this, Kate. I'll think of something."

"I'm sure you will, sir," Kate said.

"Although it's quite hard to think on an empty stomach. See if the quartermaster has any food for us, and then we'll plan what comes next."

Kate gave a short, crisp bow. "At once."

She set off across the ship, and maybe for the first few paces she did intend to follow Lord Cranston's orders. The looks the others gave her soon had her coming to a halt. They knew, even if their commander didn't, that they would be better off without her. They knew that Kate was the reason they had all been put in danger.

107

She knew it too, and in that moment, she knew what she had to do.

Kate waited until the sky started to darken before she acted. She spent the time in between running errands for Lord Cranston, and guessed that he was trying to keep her busy to take her mind off the threat to her and the others. It didn't work. Hardly a moment went past when Kate wasn't thinking about it. The others certainly were. She could see their thoughts. At least one would have thrown her over the side if he could.

Kate went to find Will. He was with his gun crew, a bandage showing the wound that he'd picked up in the battle. He, at least, smiled as he saw her approach.

"I'm surprised Lord Cranston let you come to find me," he said.

"I just wanted to see how you were," Kate said, because she couldn't tell him the truth. She couldn't tell him that she was leaving, because that would make Will complicit in what she was about to do. She couldn't risk him bearing the brunt of Lord Cranston's anger.

"It hurts a little," Will said, "but I'll be fine."

Kate smiled at the attempt at bravery, then moved closer, pulling him to her. She kissed him then, not caring who saw her. She kissed him because there might never be another chance to do it, taking as long as she could, savoring the moment.

"What was that for?" Will asked, as Kate pulled back.

"Because I care about you," Kate said, "and... well, I wanted you to know that."

And because she wanted to say goodbye, but couldn't.

"Lord Cranston will be looking for you soon," Will said.

"Yes," Kate agreed. "He will."

It took everything she had to step away from him and make it back over the deck. She had to move carefully now, slipping along to the starboard side of the ship, where one of its landing boats hung suspended by ropes. Kate worked those ropes in silence, extending her powers to feel for the attention of others and hiding whenever someone passed.

Finally, she felt the boat hit the water, and clambered down into it. Taking her sword, she sliced through the ropes holding it in place, feeling the hemp part beneath her blade and current start to take hold of the landing boat. It wouldn't be long before they missed her now. Kate knew she had to be well clear of the ship before that happened.

The question was where to go next, but the truth was that Kate had no plan beyond getting off the ship, where she would be no more danger to Lord Cranston, his company, or Will. Especially Will.

She couldn't go back toward the continent, because then she would run straight into the Master of Crows' forces. She couldn't head toward Ashton, because that was the same direction as the ship, and because that would only deliver her to the Dowager's people when she landed.

Not knowing what else to do, Kate started to row north. She would keep the others safe, whatever it took, and wherever it took her.

CHAPTER NINETEEN

Sebastian picked his way across the broken stone of the bridge as carefully as he could, trusting in the training of his horse but still wanting to push it forward. Sophia was somewhere ahead, and that thought was enough to send him hurrying across the bridge, even when his horse's hooves skittered on the broken sections.

"Not far," he told his horse, patting its neck. "We'll find her soon."

This time, it felt as though it would happen. This wasn't some feint designed to send him the wrong way. This was the right road; he knew it. Ahead he could see the estate he was heading for, while behind...

Behind, there were occasional flashes of sunlight from metal that suggested people some way behind him. Sebastian didn't know whether he was being hunted by bandits, or if it was just some traveler who happened to be heading in the same direction. Either way, the solution for him didn't change: he needed to keep going.

When he reached the estate, Sebastian found himself pausing, both admiring it and wondering why Sophia would go there. Once, it had obviously been a beautiful place. Maybe it could be again with enough work. Now, it seemed an unlikely place for anyone to come. Only the prospect of catching up to Sophia had brought Sebastian there, but that prospect was enough to send him galloping down toward the house.

No one came out to greet him, but maybe that just meant that they hadn't seen him coming. Sebastian had to hope that this wasn't another dead end, so he hopped down from his horse and led it. He walked around the house, looking for a way inside, and taking in the sheer grandeur of the place, only slightly faded with time and fire damage.

When he saw the cottage nearby, he knew that would be the place to go for answers. Where the rest of it seemed as cold and dead as a mausoleum, the cottage had smoke coming from its chimney, and a feeling of good repair that was absent in the rest. Sebastian walked the short distance to the cottage, tying his horse outside and knocking on the door.

"Sophia, are you in there?" he called. "It's Sebastian."

"She isn't here," a man's voice said, and Sebastian turned to find himself looking at a man holding a crossbow. Even as he watched, the newcomer lowered his weapon. "But if you're Sebastian, then I guess I don't need this."

"You know who I am?" Sebastian asked.

The other man nodded. "Sophia asked me to send a message for you, but if you're here now, I guess that means you aren't back in Ashton to receive it. I'm McCallum, sir. The gardener."

"What message?" Sebastian asked. He found himself thinking of what had happened back at the crossroads and hoped that this wouldn't prove to be another attempt to slow him down.

The other man shook his head. "I didn't read it. Truth is, I never did read so well. You haven't missed her by much, though."

"I haven't?" Hope started to rise inside Sebastian, but he forced himself to stay calm. "Which way did she go? Where is she?"

The gardener shrugged. "She and her friends left a little while ago. She was heading for the fishing village east of here, I think. Said something about trying to find a boat to Ishjemme."

Sebastian frowned at that. He couldn't imagine why Sophia would want to go there, to a land that was supposedly beautiful in the summer, but a frozen place for far too much of the year. It didn't matter though. All that mattered was getting to her before she left.

"I have to go," he said. "I have to catch up to her."

"Well, good luck," McCallum said. He looked past Sebastian, and Sebastian could see the fear on his face. His crossbow started to rise again. "Are they... are they with you?"

Sebastian looked around, and he suspected that his own horror matched that of the gardener. At least twenty riders were bearing down on them, and now that they were more than a half-seen flicker in the distance, he could make out the blue and gray of the royal regiments. More than that, he could identify the golden-haired figure at the front.

Rupert.

"No, they aren't," Sebastian said. "But I suspect they might be here because of me. You should get inside."

There was no time for it, though, because the riders were already there, encircling them in a ring of horses and armed men. Rupert hopped down from the saddle with casual grace, tossing his reins to one of the other men and striding forward.

"Sebastian, brother!" Rupert said, throwing his arms wide as if he might catch Sebastian up in a bear hug. "*There* you are. Mother has had me looking all over this Goddess-forsaken country for you."

"No doubt causing chaos wherever you went," Sebastian replied. "What are you doing here, Rupert?"

"Amusingly enough, I'm being the dutiful one," Rupert said. He yawned theatrically. "How *do* you do it? It's so boring. Still, here we are. Time to come home, little brother."

Sebastian shook his head. "I'm not done here. I have to find Sophia. I'm sorry, Rupert, but there's no time for this. I have to find her before she gets to the docks."

"Oh," Rupert said, looking disappointed. "And there I was thinking that you might want to spend some time with your brother." He held up a finger, as if an idea had just come to him. "Ah, there's a thought. We can hunt her down together. Mother said I had to deal with her too, so maybe you can come along while I fetch her and drag her back to Ashton in chains."

Anger flashed in Sebastian at that thought; at the thought of Rupert anywhere near Sophia.

"If you lay a finger on her—" Sebastian began, but he didn't get to finish it, because in that moment, Rupert hit him.

It wasn't a punch. Instead, it was a ringing, open-handed blow, as much insult as weapon. It was the kind of thing men used when they wanted to slap away an overenthusiastic hunting hound, or deliberately insult another to the point of a duel.

"I plan on much more than a finger," Rupert said, casually backhanding Sebastian. "And you are forgetting your place, brother. Your *place* is as the one who does all the boring things so that I don't have to. Your place is to play the dutiful prince so that I am free to do as I wish. It is not to upset Mother. It is definitely not to force me to trek across the kingdom after you."

Sebastian put a hand to his lip, tasting blood. "So what are you planning to do, Rupert? Beat me until I come to heel like a dog? Mother won't like that."

"Mother said to do whatever I needed to do to bring you back," Rupert said. "If I tell her that you tried to run, and fight, and I just *had* to hit you a few times to bring you down…" He affected a posture like an actor playing to the ring of cavalry around them. "Oh, Mother, he gave me no choice. Sebastian fought like a wild thing when I told him what I was going to do with his lady love."

To Sebastian's surprise, a figure stepped past him. McCallum the gardener had his crossbow up, this time leveled at Rupert's heart.

"That's enough," the man said. "I don't care who you are, you'll not threaten Lady Sophia!"

Sebastian tried to push back in front of the gardener. He could survive Rupert's anger, but he doubted that this man could. But it was too late. He could already see Rupert's eyes sliding to the other man, a cold look there.

"Sebastian," he said, with a tight smile. "Why don't you introduce me to your friend?"

"Leave him out of this, Rupert," Sebastian said. "It has nothing to do with him."

Rupert laughed at that.

"And what will you do to keep him safe, Sebastian?" Rupert said. "Will you come with me quietly? Will you help me to find Sophia?"

Sebastian bit his lip. "Yes."

If he did it, the gardener would live at least, and if they went to find Sophia, at least that would ensure that Sebastian was there to help her. They could escape Rupert's clutches together, if they had to.

Rupert nodded at that. "Such a noble thought."

He nodded again, and this time, it wasn't to Sebastian. The sound of a shot rang out, and McCallum gasped, clutching his shoulder. Sebastian saw his crossbow bolt flash past Rupert, missing him by a hand's breadth before flying away into the distance.

"But the fact is that I don't *want* you docile," Rupert said, as the gardener tumbled down to his knees. "And a man who threatens a prince is a traitor who deserves to die."

As if to reinforce his point, he stepped over to McCallum, drawing his slender duelist's rapier even as he stepped on the wounded man's shoulder, making him scream in agony.

"We're going to bring you back," Rupert said. "We're going to find Sophia, and we're going to make her suffer on the way back to her execution. And you know what, little brother? I'm going to make you watch every second of it."

Sebastian could feel his rage boiling up then, overwhelming any concerns he had about being surrounded by so many men, bursting through any restraints imposed by brotherly love or duty. He drew his own sword, and he threw himself at his brother.

They clashed, and the sheer momentum of Sebastian's lunge forced their blades tight together. Sebastian hit Rupert over the top of their crossed swords, then winced as Rupert's knee slammed into his thigh.

"Ah, *now* you're fighting," Rupert said with a laugh. He punched Sebastian in the ribs, once then again.

Sebastian didn't fall back under the onslaught. Instead, he brought his head back and then snapped it forward, to crash into Rupert's face. When his brother's grip loosened, Sebastian shoved him back, sending Rupert stumbling to the ground.

A part of him wanted to rush forward and continue the fight; wanted to punish Rupert for the murder he'd just committed, and the worse things he'd threatened. He wanted to plunge the sword he held into Rupert's heart, but...

...but he was his brother, and he couldn't do it. Sebastian couldn't kill his own brother. He couldn't picture having to tell his mother that he'd done it. He just couldn't bring himself to do it.

So he ran, instead, aiming for the edge of the circle of men that surrounded him. The men he ran for moved to block him, but they didn't level pistols or muskets, unwilling to risk killing a prince of the realm. Sebastian took full advantage of it, leaping at the man who was holding Rupert's horse and dragging him from the saddle. They went down in a punching, sprawling mess.

Sebastian hit the man with the hilt of his sword, catching him clumsily on the jaw, and managed to come up to his feet. He kicked out, knocking the soldier senseless, then vaulted into the saddle of his brother's horse. Another soldier moved closer, blade out now, and Sebastian slashed at him with his sword.

Then he kicked his stolen horse into a gallop and rode, bursting free of the circle of horsemen. He forced his horse forward, ignoring the sound of a shot behind him. Sebastian guessed that would be Rupert, because the others wouldn't dare to fire at him. He heard the sound of hooves behind him, and turned to see all twenty horsemen following.

"I hope you're fast," he said to the horse, bending low over its neck and forcing it forward. It would be. Rupert always insisted on the finest in everything: the most expensive tailoring, the most beautiful courtesans, the fastest horses. He wouldn't let his men ride faster beasts than he did. At least, Sebastian hoped he wouldn't.

The horse ran, and Sebastian guided it as best he could, heading for a stony hillside and picking a path up it. He reached the top of the hill and cut left, down toward a streambed flanked by a stone wall that seemed too high to consider clearing. Sebastian pushed the horse forward anyway, building up speed, and then urging it into a leap.

For a moment, he thought he'd misjudged it. He felt certain that his horse was going to crash into the stone, break a leg, send him tumbling. Instead, it seemed to hang in the air forever as it cleared the wall, its hooves splashing down in the stream. Looking back, Sebastian saw horses pulling up short at the thought of the leap. One man fell from the saddle as his horse shied away from the jump too quickly.

Sebastian knew he wouldn't have another chance. He kicked the horse forward, putting as much distance as possible between him and the chasing group of soldiers. He rode around the base of one of the nearby hills, putting them out of sight.

If he were just trying to lose them, that might have been enough. He could have picked a direction at random and set off, using the cover of Monthys's hills to make sure that they never found him again. If he did that, though, he would never find Sophia before she set off on her journey, or before his brother caught up to her. Sebastian needed to get to her, and now it was a race, because if Rupert got to her first…

Sebastian shook his head. He wouldn't let that happen.

CHAPTER TWENTY

Kate had no idea where she was, and maybe, right then, that was a good thing. Lord Cranston wouldn't be able to find her if even she didn't know where she was, and nor would the Dowager's people.

She'd pulled the boat in to shore an hour ago, dragging it up coastal scree and abandoning it in case someone came looking for her. Would they? Would they track her as a deserter now that she'd run from the company against Lord Cranston's orders? Kate didn't know. She hoped not.

Once she'd reached the coast, she headed inland. Now, she wandered a landscape that seemed to be composed mostly of peat and heather, broken only here and there by solitary trees, or small stands of them. There were mountains around, tall enough that they seemed to form the edge of the world, blotting out the possibility of anything beyond them. Kate started toward them, stopped, and looked around, simply not knowing what to do.

Was there any point in walking that way? What did she hope to find? Right then, Kate couldn't imagine hoping for anything. Hope felt like a curse, dooming her to more pain when it shattered. She'd hoped that she would feel better when she had her revenge on the House of the Unclaimed, but it had only left her feeling like ashes, and it had brought more trouble to both her and those around her. She'd hoped that she could find a life with Lord Cranston's men, but that had fallen apart as well.

Now she was alone, and Kate had never truly been alone in her life. She'd always had Sophia with her when she was young, then Thomas and Will, the company of mercenaries. Now, she was alone in a land of wind and rain that only seemed to emphasize how far Kate was from human contact.

Sophia? she sent, hoping that she could at least have that small crumb of contact. Maybe she could find out where her sister was now, and join up with her once more. For that, though, Kate needed an answer.

Sophia?

There was only silence in response. Again, it felt as though whatever small flame of hope Kate was able to summon within her ended up doused by the world. Although, out here, it might just as easily be doused by the weather. Rain was already starting to soak through her clothing, and it showed no sign of letting up anytime soon.

Kate made for one of the solitary trees, on the basis that at least it might keep her dry until she was able to work out which way she actually wanted to go. Even the tree turned out to be further than Kate hoped, forcing her to squelch her way through the boggy ground toward it as the rain continued to fall.

At least the tree provided a dry space beneath its branches, and was large enough that it was almost like sitting beneath the roof of a tent. It was an open-sided one though, and Kate huddled down into the twists and hollows at the base of the trunk, trying to keep out the wind while she waited for the weather to break. With nothing to do but sit and watch, Kate felt her eyelids fluttering closed.

Now, she was in a space that was anything but empty. Trees pressed in on all sides, and they were familiar ones, because Kate had run through them plenty of times in practice. They seemed more vibrant than they did in the waking world, though, rising to impossible heights so that they should have shut out the light. There was light, though, coming from glass jars that seemed to hold fireflies in the hundreds.

"What do you want, Siobhan?" Kate called out. She knew that she wouldn't dream of this place if there weren't a reason for it, but there *was* no good reason. She and the woman of the fountain were done. She'd repaid her debt.

There was no answer, but Kate knew the way to the fountain, even in this altered version of the wood. Her feet walked the path to it as surely as they might have in waking, while Kate watched for any sign of life in the forest. She didn't see any animals there larger than a squirrel or a small bird, but even so, she had the feeling of predatory eyes upon her, the sense of how alone she was at the heart of it all. Every step felt like an effort, and somehow, Kate knew that if she stepped off the path, something would attack her.

So she stepped off it, and found herself standing in the space where the fountain sat.

"You can be very contrary sometimes," Siobhan said, but she didn't sound displeased by it. Her fingers were trailing in the fountain, which was whole and flowing with water in the way it only seemed to be in these moments.

"You thought I'd be too scared?" Kate countered.

117

Siobhan shook her head. "Fear has never been the problem for you, has it? Anger, now... your anger has left you alone, without friends, without your sister. How does that feel, Kate?"

Kate glared back at her, willing her not to be there. "Are you in my dreams just to taunt me, Siobhan?"

She tried to work out the best way to wake up, screwing up her face with the effort of trying to bring herself back to consciousness. Nothing happened, however much she tried, and she could see Siobhan looking over with amusement.

"Your reaction is always to fight, Kate," she said. "But you need to consider where it has brought you. You have no one now."

It was uncomfortably close to what Kate had been thinking, back on the heath land. The truth was that she *did* have no one. Even when it came to her sister, there was only silence.

"I can handle being alone," Kate said.

"But is that what you want?" Siobhan asked. She looked down at the fountain's water, then back at Kate. "I asked you that once, remember? I asked you what you wanted. Well, now I'm asking again. What do you want in your life, Kate?"

Kate paused, looking around. "This is some kind of trap," she said. "You're trying to get me to make another deal with you."

"Why should I?" Siobhan asked. "You are my apprentice. I don't need any deal beyond that."

Kate set her jaw. She wouldn't let anyone simply claim her like that. She would never let anyone own her, the way the House of the Unclaimed had tried to own her.

"You're still fighting the world, Kate," Siobhan said, "but you're doing it blindly, without a hint of a real aim. What do you want? What purpose does your life have?"

A few weeks ago, Kate might have answered revenge, *had* answered that way when Siobhan asked her before. And what had that led to? To the destruction of an orphanage, the deaths of the nuns who had tormented her... and then more. It had led to the battles against the Master of Crows' New Army, to her learning of the threats that faced the kingdom.

What did she want now, knowing the consequences that might result?

"I don't know," Kate admitted. "I thought I did, but now... I don't know."

"Pick up that flower," Siobhan said, gesturing to where a lily grew on the water of the fountain, broad petals spreading across the water amidst lily pads.

Suspecting a trick of some kind, Kate moved forward cautiously, cupping her hand under the lily and lifting it from the fountain. She held it there, watching the icy white of its petals as if expecting them to strike at her.

"On the beach, when you summoned the mist," Siobhan said. "You showed me that you have access to more power than I hoped." There was a flicker of something there that might have been concern. "You managed it without my teaching, so imagine what you could do *with* it."

"Such as?" Kate said. She should have said that she wasn't interested, but the truth was that the things she'd learned from Siobhan had made her strong. They'd made it so that no one could control her again.

Siobhan laid a hand on her arm, her other hand trailing in the water of the fountain. Kate felt something shift in the world then, and it took a moment to make sense of it. It was only when she saw the corona of energy around the flower that she started to understand.

"Now, watch what happens when you draw that energy from it," Siobhan said.

Kate had the sense of something being pulled through her then, the glow around the flower diminishing as Siobhan pulled it through her. Kate had a sense of that energy joining her own, before it was pulled through her, down into the depths of the fountain. Even as she felt that, she saw the flower wither, then crumble, turning into dust.

"Imagine being able to do that to your enemies," Siobhan said.

The power there was impressive. It was also frightening enough that Kate pulled back, looking at Siobhan in the fear that it might happen to her next.

"Don't worry, Kate," Siobhan said. "I wouldn't do that to you. But there is a way you can learn if you like. Just a taste of the power you might gain if you continue your journey as my apprentice."

"You want me to learn new ways of killing the people you want dead, don't you?" Kate asked.

"Perhaps," Siobhan said. "Aren't you interested in learning more about what you can do, then?"

The truth, though, was that Kate *was* interested. Not because of the prospect of a new way to destroy, but because she'd had the sense of more inside her ever since she'd summoned the power to raise the mist on the beach.

"What would I have to do?" Kate asked.

Siobhan gestured to the fountain, its surface rippled and changed, showing mountains that seemed familiar in their outlines, because Kate had been staring at them as she fell asleep. The image moved closer, and Kate saw a path through them, culminating in a low stone hut roofed with turfs.

"There is a man who lives in the mountains," Siobhan said. "A man who showed me this skill. Your presence there provides an opportunity for you to learn from him."

"And what price will he exact from me for it?" Kate shot back. "Will he demand that I become his apprentice? Do some unnamed favor for him?"

Siobhan shrugged. "Perhaps, but there are ways to make the price less onerous."

Her hand dipped into the fountain, and it came up with a roughly circular object that seemed to have been pieced together from twigs, feathers, twine, and fallen leaves. Kate had a sense of power coming from it, and found herself wondering what it was.

"It's a map, of sorts," Siobhan said. "A collection of choices. A helping hand. Now go, Kate, and if you choose to do this, we will meet again. Wake."

Kate woke, gasping with the strength of the dream, so that it took a moment or two for her to come back to herself. She pushed back against the bark of the tree, trying to feel the solidity of it, and remind herself that *this* was real, not the dream. The dream was no more than a set of fading images in her mind.

Kate stood, looking around for the object that Siobhan had pressed into her hand, half expecting it to have somehow transferred from dream into reality. There was nothing there, though, just the image of it lingering after the dream, the twists of its feathers and twine still perfect in her memory, even as the rest of the dream started to fade.

"Just a dream," Kate told herself, but she knew that it wasn't. At least, maybe she *hoped* that it wasn't, and what had she been thinking about hope before she slept? Going after some hut in the mountains would be a foolish thing to do on the strength of it. Maybe it would be even more foolish if it turned out to be real.

She stood, looking around. The rain had stopped for now, the blue of the sky suggesting that it might stay that way for at least a little while. Around her, the heather hung with water droplets, the landscape leading up to those mountains.

All she had to do to see the path that led up into it was close her eyes. She could see the route that lay ahead, and maybe it was all a dream, but if that was all it was, she would find out soon enough.

Had she decided, then? The decision seemed almost to have come upon her without Kate realizing, but the truth was, what else was she going to do? She didn't know for certain where Sophia was, and she had no place left in Ashton or with the mercenaries.

That just left the path ahead, and the prospect of more power at the end of it. Kate could feel the need for that power inside her, as if the demonstration in the dream had roused a kind of hunger. It wasn't so much for the possibility of better ways to destroy things, as for the chance to go further with the gifts that lay inside her. Kate wanted to understand more of who she was, what she was, and to do that she needed to learn more.

Put that way, there was only one choice for her. She turned until the images of the mountains lined up with the ones she could see when she shut her eyes. Then she started to walk.

CHAPTER TWENTY ONE

Sophia couldn't believe she'd finally reached the point where she was going to have to leave her friends behind. Yet here they were, standing at a spot where the road branched, ready to do exactly that. She hesitated, not wanting the moment to pass.

Something between a fishing village and a small town sat in the distance, the coast visible now as a ribbon of blue. The other road swung onto what looked like relatively flat ground by the standards of Monthys, and both Emeline and Cora looked at it longingly.

"Are you sure you don't want to come with me?" Sophia asked. The truth was that she'd gotten used to traveling with her friends. Traveling on alone held a hint of fear she hadn't expected.

Emeline shook her head. "I want to find Stonehome. I've put it off long enough. I have to do this."

Sophia could understand that. She moved forward to hug the other girl.

"What about you, Cora?" she asked.

"I don't think I'd do well in the ice," Cora said.

Sophia hugged her too. "I guessed not. I'll miss you both. Will you be all right heading... where *are* you heading?"

"The rumors aren't clear," Emeline said. "I—"

The vision hit Sophia so sharply it hurt. She was looking down on a wide plain, dotted with standing stones. She saw clusters of stone houses, low to the ground so that they wouldn't be seen, and hidden gorges that held the promise of more. Her vision took her higher, and higher, and in that moment she *knew* where she was looking.

"The moors of the southwest," she said. "It's there."

Emeline stared at her. "You're sure?"

Sophia nodded. "I... I saw it."

She saw Emeline's eyes widen slightly at that. "You really are everything the gardener said, aren't you?"

Sophia spread her hands. "I don't know about that. I mean, you can talk mind to mind."

"And you can do a lot more than that," Emeline said. "Even I can see the difference." She paused. "If I hadn't traveled with you, I might never have known where it was."

"*We* might never have known," Cora said. She hugged Sophia again. "Thank you."

"Will you both be all right?" Sophia asked. "It's a long way, and there's no cart now."

Emeline shrugged. "So we walk, and we pick up what we can on the way. McCallum was generous, too." She hefted a burlap sack slung across her shoulder. "It feels as though I have enough food to cross a dozen kingdoms."

Despite her confidence, Sophia found herself worrying for them. It was a long walk to where they were going and now they didn't even have the cart to carry them. They'd already found out about the dangers on the road. Two young women traveling alone would be in danger at every step.

Yet the truth was that she couldn't do more than hope they would be safe.

"Promise you'll come find us in Stonehome eventually?" Cora asked.

"I promise," Sophia said, although the truth was that she had no way of knowing what would happen to her in Ishjemme, or after that. All she could do was try.

She watched her friends walking away, waving for as long as she could before she turned to Sienne, ruffling the forest cat's fur.

"It looks like it's just you and me," Sophia said, feeling Sienne press against her hand.

They turned toward the fishing village and started walking.

***

When Sophia reached the village, it was larger than she had thought it would be, but also emptier. There were plenty of buildings huddled in the sheltered bay that housed it, but many of them looked empty, and Sophia found herself remembering what McCallum had said about people leaving once her parents were no longer there to protect them.

She could see boats there, though, and they looked like sturdy things, broad and twin-masted, designed for deepwater fishing or journeys across the sea to trade. That sight gave Sophia hope that McCallum had been right, and she would be able to find passage to Ishjemme there.

She walked down into the village and headed for an inn with the sign of a leaping fish outside. Sophia guessed that captains on shore might be there, and at the very least, it would be a good place to find out who to ask.

Inside, the place fell silent in a way that had become more familiar the further north she'd gone. In a village like this, she might be one of the first outsiders they'd seen for a while, or at least, the first who'd come in overland.

What she caught of their thoughts said that it might be more than that, though.

Is she? She looks like them... no, I'm being stupid.

Strange, I must have drunk too much.

Maybe some kind of cousin...

It hadn't occurred to Sophia that in a village so close to the estate, people might recognize her for who she was. They weren't certain, of course, because even the ones old enough to have seen her parents wouldn't make the connection perfectly.

She walked over to the innkeeper, hoping that this would be a friendlier place when it came to strangers than the last inn she'd been to. Sienne's presence beside her was a comforting one, although Sophia could feel the fear coming from some of the people there.

"I'm looking for passage to Ishjemme," she said. "Do you know of any captains who are heading that way?"

The man shrugged and nodded to a man with a curling red beard and hair spiked almost at random. "Borkar trades with them."

Sophia thanked him and walked over to the trader.

"You're Borkar?" she asked.

"And you're looking to get to Ishjemme," Borkar said, his accent thick with the notes of the mountain lands. "I heard. Can you pay?"

Sophia still had the money that she'd taken from the brothers who had tried to rob her and the others on the way to Monthys, and with whom she'd gambled to get her money back. She nodded, then set out a couple of Royals on the table, hearing the clink of them as she set them down.

"I can pay." She had no idea what the going rate was for such a journey. She hoped that it would be enough.

"And is yon beastie dangerous?" he asked, nodding to Sienne.

"Very," Sophia said. "But only to people who try to hurt me."

"Fair enough," the captain said. "My ship is the one with the seahorse figurehead. We sail in two hours. If you're not there, we sail anyway."

It was enough time for Sophia to eat a little bread and cheese, tucked away in a corner of the inn where she could see out the windows. She was still doing so when she saw the riders enter the village. Her initial reaction on seeing the uniforms of the royal regiment was a rising sense of excitement, because she wanted to believe that Sebastian had come for her with a full escort, ready to be with her, his family finally happy to accept her.

She wanted to believe that. She wanted to hope that Sebastian had somehow gotten her message, even though he couldn't have in so short a time, or that he had perhaps been following behind her all this time, hoping to be with her. She hoped for it, wanted him there with her in a way she'd hoped for little else.

Then she saw Rupert dismounting from a horse, and she knew that this was anything but the joyful reunion she was hoping for. Even Sienne growled at the sight of him, although that might have been a response to the visceral combination of anger and fear that rose in Sophia at the sight of the prince there. A part of her wanted to go up to Rupert and rip him to shreds, but there were far too many men with him for that. She might succeed in killing him, but she would die horribly for it.

"Is there a back way out of here?" she asked the innkeeper.

There was, and she slipped through it with Sienne, while she heard soldiers moving toward the front of the inn, probably searching it on the basis that it was the most likely place for her to go. She needed to move quietly now. If she could get down to the docks without being seen, Rupert wouldn't even know when she left. All she had to do was—

"Going somewhere?" Rupert stepped from a side street, hand on the hilt of his sword. "I guessed that you would skulk about like a rat."

"I'd have thought that description applied more to you than to me," Sophia said. "Thankfully, I brought a cat with me."

It barely took any urging to send Sienne springing forward to slam into Rupert, knocking him to the ground. The forest cat bared her teeth, and Sophia was sure that she could rip out Rupert's throat easily, but she sent a mental pulse to call the cat back instead. She doubted Sebastian would forgive her for killing his brother.

She ran instead, with Sienne by her side, the forest cat keeping pace easily.

"She's over here!" Rupert called. "Grab her. I want her in chains!"

A soldier stepped out toward Sophia, and she shoved him away, continuing to run. She plunged down through a space where

125

fishermen were mending their nets, grabbed one, and threw it back behind her to tangle around the legs of another soldier.

She cut left, not aiming for the harbor now, because she didn't want to give away where she was heading. Instead, she pushed through the spaces between houses, changing direction rapidly, hoping to confuse the men who were behind her. One came in from the side and Sienne charged at him, bringing him down with a swipe of her claws and then running back to Sophia's side.

The forest cat leapt up a pile of low stones, onto a thatched roof. Sophia followed her, because if she stayed at ground level, it was only a matter of time before they managed to surround her. Up here, she could burrow down into the thatch and hope that they wouldn't think to look up for too long.

From here, Sophia could see the soldiers making their way around the village. Some burst into houses, others hurried around the streets, trying to run her down through sheer effort. Rupert stood at the heart of it all, yelling orders and threats almost in equal measure.

"I want her found!" he yelled. "I want her brought to me. Sophia, can you hear me?"

She wasn't going to be stupid enough to answer.

"We're going to find you, Sophia, and I am going to drag you back to the capital behind my horse, wearing nothing but the skin of that beast of yours. At every place we stop, I'm going to put you on display for the people to see, and every time we make camp, I will find a new way to torture you. By the time we get back to Ashton you will beg, *beg* to be executed!"

Sophia had no doubt that he meant it. She'd seen firsthand the kind of cruelty Rupert was capable of. The thought of that was enough to make her wish that she had let Sienne finish him, but if she'd done that, they would never stop chasing her.

Not that it looked as though they would do so now. Men were already moving among the houses, one walking almost directly below Sophia's hiding place. She held her breath, one hand on Sienne's head in a signal to the forest cat to remain silent. The man passed by, and Sophia dared to breathe again.

The soldiers' horses were over by the inn. Perhaps if she could get to one of them…

No, that wouldn't work. Even if she could somehow ride faster than a company of cavalry, it left her going in the wrong direction. Sophia wouldn't be able to get to Ishjemme, wouldn't meet her uncle, and wouldn't find out what had happened to her parents after the night when the killers had come.

Still, it gave her an idea. She reached out with her powers, feeling for the minds of the horses in the way that she'd found Sienne's mind. She could sense them now, well trained but still skittish under that exterior. Sophia built on that skittishness, feeding their fear, then taking an image of Sienne and throwing it at them.

They reared and bucked, then finally broke free of the sloppily tied reins holding them. Sophia gave them the sense of the forest cat following behind them, and now they ran from the village, charging back up the path into the wild spaces beyond.

Below her, she saw the soldiers milling about, trying to make sense of it all, and Sophia decided to take a risk.

"Quick!" she called out, doing her best to imitate the rough tones of a soldier. "She's getting away!"

Now they ran, chasing after the horses. None of them seemed to know quite what was going on, but from the thoughts that she could see, all of them assumed that one of the others had seen a glimpse of her among the fleeing horses. Even Rupert took off in the direction they'd gone, running awkwardly in boots better suited to riding.

Silently, Sophia slipped down from the roof, with Sienne following in her wake. She knew that her distraction would only buy her a limited amount of time, and once Rupert worked out that he'd been fooled, he would be back, angrier than ever, ready to kill anyone who got in his way.

She needed to get to the boat, so she hurried down through the village toward the harbor.

CHAPTER TWENTY TWO

The Master of Crows stood impassively, while around him, his captains gathered. So many captains. Another man might have been proud of an army that size.

"The clear up on the beach is progressing well, sir," Klathard said. He was a large, dark-skinned mercenary who had joined the New Army when his side had lost a battle ten years ago. "The burnt vessels are out of the way now."

"And the ones for the invasion?" he asked.

"Loading proceeds apace," Van Jord replied. He had joined his ships to the force when the New Army had taken his city.

"See that it is done faster," the Master of Crows said. "In war, the side that moves fastest wins most often."

They hung on his words, of course. One, Haddet, even wrote them down as though planning a monogram on his general's genius. The Master of Crows had no time for it. He had seen death, and everything else felt like dust.

So many men, from so many lands, so many sides, all absorbed into his New Army. So long as they fed his crows with the energy of the dying, the Master of Crows didn't care where they came from.

"What else?" he asked. He could have seen for himself, of course. He could have reached out and seen through the eyes of any corvid he wanted, but sometimes it was easier to ask.

"I have sent men to clear the bodies from the beach," K'tha said. He hadn't even been part of the wars on the continent. He had simply come in from Morgassa to fight when he had heard about the scale of the conquest on offer.

"Leave them," the Master of Crows said. "Let the crows feast."

He had been the one they'd been feasting on once, after a spear had taken him in a battle so long ago that the world barely remembered it now. They had come for him and he had reached out for them with a talent he hadn't known he had until then.

He'd lost his name in that moment, but it hadn't mattered.

There had been many more battles since then, and many more crows. The Master of Crows had found that the speed and power others' energy gave him was an advantage, but not as much as being able to see through the eyes of all corvids, knowing exactly where his foes were, and what their plans would be.

"You should be aware, my lord, that one of the gifted has been captured," Captain Var said. He'd joined them after being part of a force sent to bring them down by one of the churches after they'd declared him anathema. He'd maintained the skills used in hunting the talented, but now he did it for more useful purposes.

"Show me," the Master of Crows replied, half hoping that it would be the girl he had fought on the beach. But no, that one would not be taken so easily by his men. Siobhan's pet was a more powerful thing than that.

Even so, any of the gifted was a good thing. Their essence fed the crows better than anything.

"You have a talent," the Master of Crows said.

"And so you think you're going to declare me some kind of heretic or witch?" the man countered.

The Master of Crows laughed bitterly at that. "You have me confused with some servant of the Masked Goddess. Would you like to live? Are your skills useful ones to add to my army?"

"You tell me," the farmer said, and lashed out with a burst of mental power that would have been quite impressive against anyone else. The Master of Crows had the full power of his crows behind him, though, all the energy they had taken with their feeding, and he brushed the attempt off.

"Take him and put him in a gibbet," he said. He'd found that power lingered longer while the talented were alive. The crows could feed for longer, and they always needed feeding.

How long had he been feeding them now? Fifty years? More than that? It was impossible to say for sure. His face didn't show the years, but only because of the constant swell of power from all corners of his growing empire as the crows did their grim work.

For now, he let his attention flicker between sets of eyes wherever he could find them. One flew on the edge of desert sands, hunting for carrion in a space where monuments almost as old as humanity stood half buried. Another flew over ice, watching bears hunting in the snow that formed a barrier between there and Ishjemme. He watched a dozen cities, some still in the process of being taken, some held in the grip of harsh laws that promised a feast for the crows, one in the middle of being razed as an example.

He found himself thinking again about the girl he'd fought on the beach. She'd had skill, and she'd had power, enough to feel like a threat for what seemed like the first time in forever. His plans had taken into account the magic of things like Siobhan, and the other known powers of the island, but this had been an unexpected addition. He still wasn't sure what to make of it.

"Crow food," he told himself. "I'll make crow food of them all."

He walked back toward the edge of the town, where his army was gathering, its ochre uniform a reminder of a time when those had truly been his colors. His captains followed him, waiting for his orders, trusting him with a faith that bordered on the religious. None of them seemed to understand that he would see them dead as easily as his enemies.

"Are the men prepared?" he asked.

"They will fight with the strength of true warriors!" Captain Namas said. He was one of the newer ones. The Master of Crows still wasn't sure if he would last.

"I have no time for warriors," he said. "I want obedient soldiers, not heroes. Will they march where I tell them, die if I tell them? Will you?"

"In a heartbeat," the captain said.

The Master of Crows cocked his head to one side. "Then prove it. Take a knife and kill yourself." He fixed his captain with a level gaze, then handed him a blade. "Now."

The other man laughed. "You... I was speaking figuratively, my lord."

The Master of Crows nodded and took the blade back, then thrust it through the other man's chest so fast he probably didn't even see it.

"I was not."

He stood there, watching his captain fall. He considered simply letting him die, but the crows had been fed well by the battle, and he was feeling generous. He pushed energy into the wound, closing it as easily as he'd caused it. Captain Namas gasped, looking shocked as he found that he could breathe again.

"When I give a command, you will follow it," the Master of Crows said.

"Yes, my lord."

The Master of Crows could hear now that his captain would. He *believed* now.

The Master of Crows didn't care. He didn't need belief, so long as the men fed the crows, and through them, him. So long as they gave him the power to keep going. That was the part that mattered. Anything else was ephemeral. The Master of Crows looked down at them, seeing the numbers there, and the determination.

He suspected the Dowager's kingdom would feed him well.

CHAPTER TWENTY THREE

Kate found herself looking around every few strides through the mountains, unwilling to believe that she might really be on the right path. Nevertheless, the details seemed to line up with her dream almost exactly. There were boulders and overhangs in the same places, the path twisting to the same degree. Kate kept following it, still not sure if she was doing the right thing.

She took another step forward, and fear and pain hit her like a hammer.

It came out of nowhere, there one step after there had been nothing. There was terror such as Kate had never experienced in her life, coupled with pain that felt like she was rolling in stinging nettles, or set on fire. The sheer shock of it made her recoil, and as she did so, Kate felt the sensation fade, gone as quickly as it had come.

She took a step forward again, and the screaming agony was there once more.

Kate stepped back, trying to work out what was happening. There was no sign of anything there beyond a faint shimmer in the air, but even that told her something: this was some kind of barrier. Siobhan had done something similar to her once in the forest. So, how did she get through it? There was only one answer that Kate could see.

She stepped forward again.

She couldn't ignore the pain, but was it worse than the endless pain she'd endured in the House of the Unclaimed? Was it worse than feeling blades sliding into her endlessly as Siobhan trained her to fight? Was the fear worse than the times when she'd been in battle? Step by step, Kate forced herself forward across the rocky ground.

Finally, the pain and the fear disappeared, leaving only the crisp air of the mountains, and the soft gravel of the path ahead. Kate stood there, letting the agony pass from her body, feeling her muscles relax after cramping so hard with pain. It took long minutes before Kate felt able to keep walking.

There was a bend in the track ahead. Around it...

It was strange, seeing reality match her dreams so exactly. Strange, and a little frightening as she looked at the low stone cottage there, ringed by plants that seemed to be surviving in spite of the harsh environment of the mountains. If this much was true, then the rest might be as well. This really might be the place for her to learn the horrific power Siobhan had shown her.

Was that really what Kate wanted?

She didn't have an answer to that, but she also didn't have anywhere better to go, so she started forward toward the cottage's door. It swung open as she got close, but no one stepped out to meet her. Kate stepped inside, knocking on the wooden frame of the door even though it was obvious someone was expecting her.

"Hello?" she said. "Is anyone there?"

"Was the barrier not enough of a hint?" a man's voice demanded.

The interior of the cottage was a cluttered place, as if the contents of some much larger space had been crammed down into it. There were boxes and scrolls, flasks and beakers, plants in jars and pots.

The man who stood at the heart of it all was bent over with age, his hair and beard both white and unkempt. He wore robes that looked more like a scholar's than a priest's, while crabbed hands seemed to be in ceaseless motion by his side.

"Well?" he demanded. "Are you going to tell me who you are, and what's so important that you clambered through my mountains, then fought your way past my barrier?"

His mountains. There was something about the way he said it that reminded Kate of the way Siobhan talked about her woods.

"My name is Kate," she said. "Siobhan sent me to learn from you."

"Ah," he said, and his expression changed. It was no longer irritable, but now there was a note of wariness there instead. "That is a name I haven't heard in years."

A part of Kate wanted to ask how many years, because this man had a look of age to him that Siobhan didn't show. Of course, Kate already knew that Siobhan was far older than she appeared.

"I am Finnael, though most of the farmers out this way call me Old Finn, if they remember me at all. If you are from her, and you are here to learn, then you will have something for me."

He stood there expectantly, and Kate had the sense that this was as much a test as the barrier had been.

"Siobhan gave me something in a dream," Kate said, "but it wasn't there when I woke."

"Perhaps it was just a dream then," Finnael said. "Siobhan knows the price of my help. I told her a long time ago, and she is not one to forget. Strange that such a thing would fade though."

Kate frowned at that, and then a thought came to her. What if she didn't need a physical version of the object Siobhan had passed to her? Siobhan had said that it was a representation, a collection of choices given form. Could Kate remember it?

She reached for the memories of the dream, and found that while the rest of it was starting to fade, the moment where Siobhan had passed the object to her remained, as clear as in the moment when Kate had first seen it. She found that if she concentrated, she could see every detail of the twigs and leaves, twine and feathers. She could turn it around in her mind, so that she could see it from angles she was sure she hadn't in the dream.

On impulse, she took the image and sent it across in Finnael's direction using her talent.

"Ah," he said, and Kate saw his expression change again. He seemed pleased now, and a little surprised. "I never thought that she would give me this. This must matter a great deal to her."

He stood there, and Kate could imagine him turning the image over in his mind, examining it from every angle. She didn't dare look, in case he took that as an insult. She did, however, step forward after a while to put a hand on his arm, if only because it seemed that he had forgotten her.

"Is it the right payment?" she asked.

"It is," Finnael admitted. "And I imagine that there is only one skill that Siobhan will have sent you to me to learn."

He lifted a plant, and just as in her dream, Kate saw it wither as the energy was pulled from it.

"I take it that is what you wish to learn?"

"I…" Kate hesitated, because she still wasn't sure if this *was* what she wanted. She had a horrible feeling that this was part of some plan of Siobhan's, and she had no doubt that if her would-be teacher was giving her a better way to kill, it was only so that she could do it on command. How many more like Gertrude Illiard would there be if she accepted this?

"You don't seem certain," Finnael said. "Could it be that Siobhan has found herself an apprentice with a conscience?"

Kate swallowed, unsure if he meant that as an insult or a compliment. Maybe that was the point. Maybe this was another test. In any case, Kate knew there was only one answer that she wanted to give.

"I don't like being just a cog in Siobhan's plans," Kate said, "even if I am supposed to be her apprentice. What use is this power, except to murder people?"

Finnael nodded at that, then moved over to another plant that looked to be wilting.

"It is a good question, and one that Siobhan didn't bother asking when I showed her this," Finnael said.

"Why not?" Kate asked.

"Maybe she didn't need more. Maybe she was just so talented with this that she could work the rest out for herself. She certainly seems to have learned to manipulate the energies of her domain." Finnael sighed. "Maybe she didn't see the use in something that wasn't a weapon."

Kate could imagine that. Even so, she wanted more from this than just another way to kill. She saw Finnael touch the partly wilted plant, and she felt the power going into it. To her shock, she saw the leaves of the plant become green, the stem straightening.

"The power to manipulate life energy can heal as well as kill," the old man said. "It is not just about taking, but about moving power, even giving it if you are willing to take the consequences."

In an instant, Kate knew that he hadn't always looked like that.

"I still don't understand," she said. "How does all this work?"

"It will vary," Finnael said. "Each of us has things we can connect to, things that are ours to manipulate. Places that become foci for power, mediums that they like to work with, whether water, or fire, or blood. For me, it is the things that come onto this mountain. For Siobhan, it is the land around that fountain of hers. I take it you have drunk from it?"

Kate nodded. She could still remember that first taste.

"Perhaps not a wise move, considering what she can do with it."

Kate didn't want to think about that. She'd already seen enough of what Siobhan could do, given the fates of those who had crossed her. She'd seen them, screaming in the depths of it.

"So I could learn to tie myself to a mountain so that I can learn to revive plants?" Kate asked.

She saw Finnael shrug. "It might not be like that for you. As I said, it varies for everyone who learns it. Once, there were those who could draw on the powers of whole kingdoms, or the congregations of the old gods. But that was a long time ago."

Even so, Kate wasn't sure that she wanted this.

"If Siobhan has asked you to do this, I suspect there will be a reason," Finnael said. "I do not have her talent with the futures—if I did, I wouldn't need what you gave me—but I can attempt to see *some* things."

He led Kate over to a spot where a mirror stood, covered with a cloth embroidered with the constellations, the Hawk and the Mask, the Stones and the Scales of Balance.

"If I can see out, others can see in," he explained without being asked. "Now, look deep, and tell me what you see."

Kate frowned, sure that there should be more to it than that. Even so, she looked, staring at her reflection, then looked deeper, trying to stare through the glass. She could feel power coming from Finnael beside her, but more than that, she could feel her own powers rising up from within.

The image in the mirror shifted, and she saw Sophia asleep somewhere. No, Kate realized with a start, not asleep. She was too pale for that, too still, and her chest wasn't rising with breath. A wound in her chest spoke of violence. She was on a boat somewhere that Kate didn't recognize, the port outside not one that Kate had seen before.

Almost as soon as it had come, the image faded, leaving Kate staring and hoping that she'd seen it wrong.

"She can't be dead. She can't," Kate said.

Beside her, Finnael shrugged. "Remember that this is just a glimpse of what could be. No one can show you more than that."

"But this... this will happen if I do nothing?" Kate asked. "When? Where?"

Again, Finnael spread his hands. "This is not my strength, so I would guess soon. Where is easier. There is a fishing village an hour's hard ride away to the south. I buy food there sometimes."

Kate turned toward the door, ready to see how fast she could run.

"I would also guess that the power to heal would be useful in such a situation," Finnael said.

Kate knew that he was right. She needed to learn, if she was going to save her sister. Yet there might not be any time. For all Kate knew, the things she'd seen might happen at any moment.

"How quickly can you teach me?" Kate asked.

"How quickly can you learn?" Finnael countered.

He stood, motioning for her to join him, and picked another plant.

"Can you see the energy there?" he asked. "Can you feel it?"

"I... don't know," Kate admitted.

He had her hold it, then pulled power through her, drawing it from the plant and then pushing it back in while Kate tried to watch

135

the movement of it all. She could feel it, she realized, and do more than that, because now she could see the faint glow of it around the plant. She noted that the plant was still slightly brown and wilted by the end of the process.

"Why isn't it as green as it was?" she asked.

"The process isn't perfect," Finnael explained. "It takes more life than was lost to restore a thing. You try now."

Kate tried, but even though she could feel the energy around the plant, she couldn't quite grasp it.

"Again," Finnael instructed.

"I have to get to Sophia before—"

"*Again*. And this time don't focus on just the plant. Feel for what your domain will be, or your conduit. Feel what connection you will need."

Kate reached for the plant's energy once more, trying to feel it, and understand it. She let herself spread out, and in that moment, she felt vastness all around her. She felt grass and hills, rivers and moors. It felt far too immense to be the kind of domain Finnael was describing.

Even so, she found that she could draw energy from it; just a fragment of the whole, sending it out into the plant she held. She looked up as the weight in her hand increased, and to her astonishment saw that the flower had grown into something twice the size.

She wasn't the only one looking astonished. Across from her, the old man was standing there looking as though everything he'd just seen was impossible.

"But that…" Finnael began. "The last ones who could do that were…"

Kate shook her head. She had no time for his astonishment. "Have I done it? Do I have what I need to save my sister?"

She saw the old man nod, and that was all she needed. Perhaps she stood have stood there long enough to thank him or learn what he had to say. Right now, though, there was only one thing she could think about: her sister was in danger, and now she had the power to save her.

Kate sped away with all the speed her powers gave her, hoping that she would be in time.

CHAPTER TWENTY FOUR

Sophia searched frantically for the boat with the seahorse at its prow, knowing that she only had so much time before Rupert and the others realized they had been tricked and came back to search the harbor properly.

She scoured the boats there, ignoring the tiny fishing vessels too small to ever risk making such a crossing and the boats that clearly showed other signs. There were still enough large vessels, however, that she had to hurry among them, looking them over and hoping that this one, or that one, might prove to be the one she needed.

She needed to find the ship, because she needed to get to Ishjemme. She needed to find her uncle. What would it be like once she did? First, she suspected that she would need to persuade him that she was who she claimed to be, because a man with that kind of position would be wary of imposters. After that... she didn't know.

It was simply too hard to imagine the idea of having some kind of a family again beyond her sister, even if it was just an uncle she couldn't even remember. Or could she? If Sophia concentrated, she thought she could bring to mind an image of a man with the same red hair as her mother, who had seemed happy to laugh and play at being soldiers with Kate.

Was that her uncle, or was she just constructing an image to fill in an empty space? Even if that was him, could Sophia really expect that he would have stayed the same after so long? People changed, especially when they found themselves in the middle of difficult circumstances.

Sophia tried to push down her hope, but even so, it was impossible not to feel it. She wanted this to be true. She wanted to find her uncle, and after that... that part was almost too much to think about. Would her uncle know what had happened to her parents?

Finally, she saw a seahorse larger than a man affixed to the front of a ship. The vessel had two masts, and a bank of thick oars that would be useful in rivers. Most of its hull had been painted a mixture of blue and gold, so that the seahorse swirled with the colors; even the sails showed the same sign.

When she came closer, Sophia saw that Borkar was up on deck, supervising the loading of the ship. He didn't look as relaxed as he had back at the inn, and one glance at his thoughts said that he was planning on leaving as soon as his ship was fully laden.

"You're planning to leave without me?" Sophia asked.

He turned, looking down from the rail of the ship at her. He jabbed a finger back in the direction of the village.

"Are you the reason why there were soldiers from the queen's own regiment wandering around the village?" he demanded.

Sophia thought about lying, but how could she, when she was the only new person in the village, and Rupert had been shouting his threats to her for anyone to hear?

"Yes," she admitted, "but that just means I need to get out of here as much as you do."

She saw the captain shake his head.

"Not on my ship you don't," he said. "I've no love for those royal scum, but I'll not give them an excuse to burn my ship with me and my crew on it."

That answer hit Sophia as surely as a punch might have. She'd been sure that once she made it to the ship, she would be safe. She'd paid for her passage, so she'd assumed that it represented a bolt hole for her in the face of Rupert's attempts to capture her. To be told that Borkar wouldn't carry her on his ship felt like having that safety ripped away all at once.

Maybe there was a time when Sophia would have stood for that. Now, though, she needed this too much. She clambered onto the ship, pulling herself over the railings to confront the captain. Sienne leapt up beside her, landing lightly.

"I told you," he said. "There's no place for you here."

"You were quick enough to take my money," Sophia pointed out.

"I'll return every Royal to you," Borkar replied. "But I'll not risk getting into a fight with a full squad of soldiers for some girl I don't even know."

Sophia thought about offering more money, offering anything the captain wanted, if only he would take her across the sea as he had promised. She looked into his thoughts, trying to work out what would sway him, and what she found surprised her. He wasn't just angling for more money.

I can't risk my boys. If I give the Dowager's thugs a reason to attack, they will. They've no love for me. And then I won't be able to keep working to bring the kingdom back to what it should be. I can't risk all that for one girl.

"You're working against the Dowager?" Sophia said.

Instantly, there was a knife in the captain's hand. Beside Sophia, Sienne growled.

"Who told you that?" the captain said. "Give me one reason I shouldn't kill you and throw you in the bay."

"No one told me," Sophia said. "I read it in your thoughts."

It was a big thing to give away, but right then Sophia suspected it was only the shock of something like that which would persuade the captain to help her.

"In my…" That seemed to be enough to make the captain pause. "Is that why you're seeking passage then? You're trying to get out of the kingdom before the Masked Goddess's priests get to you? I can sympathize with that, but there are a dozen directions you could run in. You don't need to be on my ship."

If I'm caught with her, they'll tear the boat apart. They'll find the letters I'm carrying, and it will be over.

"I don't need to go in a different direction," Sophia insisted. "I need to get to Ishjemme. There are things there I have to find."

"And what is there for you in Ishjemme?" Captain Borkar asked.

She's hiding something. Well, I have no more time for lies. It's the truth, or she goes in the bay, and may all the gods forgive me.

"My uncle is there," Sophia said. She knew she had to say the next part, but she still hesitated, because there were things that couldn't be unsaid. "Lars Skyddar."

She's joking. She's lying. Duke Lars's nieces are long dead.

"We survived," Sophia said, answering his thoughts as much as a reminder that she could as because she thought he needed the explanation. "I am Sophia Danse, daughter of Lord Alfred and Lady Christina Danse."

He stared at her in disbelief, then something like shock.

It can't be… but she has the look of them. That hair, those features. And she has their talents.

"You could be an imposter," he said. "There are other red-haired girls in the world, and the eye sees what it wants when it comes to family resemblances. There are even plenty of those with power in the world."

"And why would I pick that one lie out of all the ones I could have chosen?" Sophia countered. "It might keep me safe for now, but it puts me in more danger later on. I can't imagine that Lars Skyddar would react well to an imposter."

139

She has a point. She might be deluded, but the resemblance is uncanny. Which means…

She saw the captain fall to one knee, moving with surprising grace despite his size.

"Your highness," he said. "Please forgive me. I would never have threatened you had I known who you truly were."

A part of Sophia wanted to sigh in relief at the suddenness of the reversal. She was safe now, after all. Even so, Sophia shook her head. "That shouldn't have mattered. I shouldn't have to be some kind of princess before you agree to help me. What about the next girl, or the next?"

She saw him redden at that, but not with anger. She could feel the shame coming off him.

"You're right," Captain Borkar said. "Please, accept my apology. I and mine have always been loyal to the true rulers of this kingdom. Please allow me to see you to safety."

Sophia could see that he would stay kneeling there until she did something, so she put her hands on his shoulders, pulling him up to his feet.

"I just want to see my uncle," she said. "If you can get me there safely, I'll forgive just about anything."

He nodded, then turned to his crew. "Right, lads, hurry up. No, leave that, we've a more precious cargo. Princess Sophia Danse is aboard today."

Sophia winced as he said it, because she had no idea if declaring it to the world would simply place her in more danger. To her surprise, the sailors crewing the vessel reacted in almost the same way their captain had: they stopped what they were doing and fell to one knee, their heads bowed almost in reverence.

"Tell them to stand up," Sophia said. "I don't deserve this."

"You deserve this and more if you are who you claim," Borkar said.

"But it also says to anyone watching that there is someone important aboard," Sophia pointed out.

"Hmm, you have a point, your highness. Get back about your work, you lazy dogs!" Borkar gestured to the stern of the ship, where a cabin stood up from the deck. "We should also get you out of sight. My cabin will keep you from prying eyes."

Sophia followed him, with Sienne in her wake. The cabin was small and obviously designed more for practicality than comfort, but still far more comfortable than any of the spaces she'd slept in when she was in the House of the Unclaimed. There was a bed, a shelf with maps and logbooks set out on it, and a broad trunk that could have contained anything.

For the first time since she'd reached the village, Sophia started to think that things might turn out well. She had a way to get to her uncle. She'd lost Rupert and his men. She knew where she was going. Even the days of walking for hours on end were over now, because the ship meant that she could simply wait, and rest, and watch the world that could be seen through the cabin's small window.

Through it, she saw Rupert and his men returning on foot, their horses long gone. Apparently, Captain Borkar had seen the same thing.

"Damn it. They're coming for the docks. Stay out of sight, and I'll deflect them. We just have to hope that they've not talked to anyone at the inn, or it will be a fight after all."

Sophia crouched down near the window, trying to find an angle from which she could see outside without being seen. She extended her gifts as far as she could, picking up the anger of Rupert's thoughts as he stormed across the docks.

The good news was that he didn't come straight for their vessel, as they would have done if they knew for sure where Sophia was hiding. Instead, they moved from ship to ship, house to house, looking inside and moving on.

She felt the moment when Rupert came aboard in Captain Borkar's thoughts. He was considering reaching for a weapon, wondering whether he would have to fight.

"What can I do for you, your highness?" he boomed as Rupert came aboard. It probably came across to Rupert as bucolic joviality, but Sophia knew that it was a warning to her to hide.

"You can tell me if any young women have tried to get aboard your ship," Rupert snapped.

"There was one, your highness, but when I saw that your men were searching, I told her that I didn't want to be involved. I thought about grabbing her, but that creature she had with her…"

"A wise choice," Rupert said. "Which way did she go?"

"That way, I think, your highness."

"And you won't mind me checking your boat to make sure that she isn't here?"

Again Sophia felt the tension in the captain. For her part, she dove under the bed in the cabin, urging Sienne to join her. The forest cat pressed against her as they hid.

"I am at your command, your highness," Borkar said. "As you can see, there aren't many places she could be aboard a vessel like this."

"What about that cabin?"

Sophia heard the creak of the door opening, and she could feel Borkar's tension building.

If he sees her, I'll kill him, and damn the consequences.

She heard Rupert's booted feet on the deck. Would he actually search the room? If he did, she had no doubt that he would find her, because her hiding place was pitiful. She could feel Rupert's thoughts, filled with anger and hate. She took a risk, pushing a thought Rupert's way.

She's getting away. I'm wasting time.

She held her breath.

"It seems you were telling the truth," Rupert said. "Which way did you say she went, Captain?"

"That way, your highness."

"Then if I catch her, I'll see you rewarded."

Sophia heard the sound of Rupert's boots retreating, and dared to pull herself out from under the bed. Captain Borkar was there waiting for her.

"By the old gods, I thought I was going to have to knife a prince."

"It wouldn't be much of a loss to the world," Sophia assured him. "But we don't have much time now."

"Aye," he agreed. "Sooner or later, he'll realize that no one saw you after you came to my ship. Someone will tell him the truth. Better if we're not here when that happens."

He hurried out onto the deck, issuing orders once again. For her part, Sophia dared to relax. Rupert might still be searching for her, but for now at least, the danger was past, she was safe, and soon she would be with her uncle.

CHAPTER TWENTY FIVE

Angelica stood in a small stand of trees and watched the harbor with the stillness of a snake waiting to strike. She'd been watching for more than an hour now, forcing herself to remain calm, waiting for her moment. Someone else might have found that hard, or given in to the urge to rush down there, but Angelica knew how to be patient.

She'd watched Sophia's arrival in the village, watched her walk around, obviously seeking passage to Ishjemme, as she'd said in her letter. Angelica had considered striking at her in the streets of the village, stepping out from a doorway or ambushing her in the inn, but the truth was that there were too many people there for that. She might be able to do what she needed to and get away, but people would see her, and that would mean that they talked.

It was funny that she was more afraid of getting caught than of the prospect of killing Sophia. Angelica found that was often the way of things. When she had to ruin some rival or bribe some official, she knew that most people would declare themselves disgusted by the thought of such an act. Angelica only worried about what might happen to her if she weren't careful.

"And I'm always careful," Angelica said, as she stretched and stood up.

When Rupert had come, she'd thought perhaps that he might do her job for her. Certainly, the way he'd been shouting had suggested that he had murder in mind by the end of it. Angelica could have ended things then simply by walking up to him and telling him where Sophia was hidden. She'd seen her hiding, after all, first on the roof, then in the boat.

She hadn't called out for three reasons. First, it would have told people that she was involved in this, and that would have complicated things with Sebastian too much when he inevitably heard the rumors. No one could see her here.

Second, there was always a danger in being around Rupert, especially in a place as remote as this. He would undoubtedly propose that they travel back together, and Angelica had no wish to have to barricade her door against him at night.

143

The third reason was the most important one: she wanted to see the moment when Sophia died and all of this ended. For that, Angelica was willing to do far more than simply give her rival away.

Now, looking down at the harbor, she could see the situation was as perfect as it was going to get. There were men around on the ship, but Sophia appeared to be alone in the cabin. Rupert was off at the other end of the village, questioning people. If Angelica waited much longer, there was also the danger that the boat would simply leave.

"It's time," Angelica said to herself. She tied her horse in place using a sapling, then started to creep down along the shoreline. She kept the hood of her cloak up as high as she could manage, considering the best way to get aboard the vessel where Sophia was hiding. Could she walk up and claim to be her friend? Try to book passage? Sneak up the gangplank? All of those seemed like recipes for disaster.

When she found a small rowing boat, Angelica knew what she had to do, pushing the vessel into the water and taking its oars in delicate hands. Ordinarily, she had no need to row; on the occasions when she found herself on a river, it was because some swain was trying to impress her with his strength, or there was a servant to do the hard work. Now, Angelica pulled herself through the still water, her muscles straining with the effort.

She aimed for the stern of the ship, on the basis that it was where the cabin sat. She knew she would have to cross the deck at some point, but the more she could minimize it, the better. It would mean fewer people to see her, and less chance of being caught.

They might kill her if they caught her, here in the north where no one knew who she was. The thought of that brought a twinge of fear, but also the determination to do this properly.

It seemed to take an age to reach the ship, and by the time she did, Angelica was sweating with the effort. She wasn't done yet, though. Tying the fishing boat to the larger vessel, she picked one of the lines running buoys down into the water and started to climb.

Her journey across the country had made her stronger. Even so, it took most of her strength to pull herself over the railing of the boat. She slipped aboard, moving as quietly as she could as she made her way down toward the door where—

"What are you doing there?"

Angelica turned, seeing a young sailor there, looking at her as if uncertain whether to make a grab for her or call for help. Angelica smiled.

"I'm here to see Sophia," she said. "I'm here to help her."

To help her into the next world, at least.

"Who are you?" the young man demanded, while Angelica's hands considered the various objects at her belt. There was no time to arrange poison, and the close confines of the boat meant that the pistols she'd taken from the bandits were out of the question. Even her knives would take a moment or two to get to, too long if he decided to call out.

"I'm Sophia's friend," Angelica said, moving closer, remembering that there had been others with her on the road. "I traveled with her most of the way, but was going to go in a different direction. Now, seeing that she gets to travel with such big strong men, I've changed my mind."

It was overdoing things, of course, but Angelica didn't have time for subtlety. She just needed to get closer.

The sailor boy still looked confused, but that didn't matter, because at that point, Angelica spotted a belaying pin tangled in the ropes, waiting to hold them fast. Angelica snatched it and struck, catching him on the side of the head so that he dropped like a stone.

Angelica pushed him back as he fell, forcing him to the rail and then over it, putting all the effort into it that she had. He tumbled, falling into the harbor with a splash and vanishing from sight almost immediately. Angelica didn't know if she'd killed him with that first blow or not, but it didn't matter. What mattered was that he wouldn't surface to say that she'd been there.

She turned her attention to the cabin door, staying crouched so that no one would see her. Testing the handle, she found that it wasn't locked, which struck her as foolish. She had time to draw a stiletto now, so she did, taking a moment or two to coat its blade with essence of foxglove, so that there would be no mistake about this. She also palmed a small bag.

Angelica pushed the door open and stepped inside, only to be greeted by the growl of the great cat that lay in front of the bed. Sophia was there too, looking at Angelica with obvious surprise.

"What are you doing here?" she asked.

"I'm here because I have a message from Sebastian," Angelica said.

Sophia was already shaking her head by the time Angelica finished saying it.

"I can see your thoughts, Angelica. I know that isn't what you're here to do."

See her...

145

"You're more than just some indentured slut, then," Angelica said. "You're an abomination too."

It was just one more reason to hate Sophia. It wasn't that Angelica cared much for the strictures of the Masked Goddess, but anyone who could see into her head and ferret out her secrets was to be despised. If Angelica had known, she would have poisoned Sophia when she first met her, just to be safe.

"And you're here to kill me," Sophia said, her expression still caught in surprise at it all. "Why, Angelica? Why would you do such a thing?"

"You don't get to call me Angelica, you imposter, you *owned thing*," Angelica snapped back. "You came into my life and disturbed everything. I could have been married to Sebastian by now, but instead, the Dowager has me traveling the length of the country, making sure that you can't be a threat."

"She sent you as well as Rupert?" Sophia said. "She must be getting desperate if she's resorting to you as an assassin."

"That's how much Sebastian means to her," Angelica said. "And to me. You have no right to interfere with the affairs of your betters like that."

"My betters?" Sophia said, and for some reason, she laughed again. "You really have no idea what this is really about, do you? You think it's just about Sebastian."

Right then, Angelica wished that she were the one able to read minds, because it was obvious that there was something Sophia was keeping from her.

"What is it about then?" Angelica demanded.

Sophia shook her head. "I'm not giving you any more ammunition against me. Tell me this, do you love Sebastian at all?"

Angelica wondered what the point of that question was. She considered Sebastian a good match, handsome and likely to be a good husband, even before the obvious advantages of his position were considered. There was a reason she was pursuing him rather than Rupert. Even so, what place did love have in an affair such as this? Love was for the lower orders.

"Is that it?" Sophia demanded, and again, Angelica had the feeling that she'd plucked the thoughts from her head like some kind of thief.

"Better a thief than a murderer," Sophia snapped. "Although I'm wondering how you plan to do it. Sienne."

The forest cat stood, poised to pounce, its teeth bared in an obvious threat as it hissed.

"Even if it were the two of us, I could probably beat you," Sophia said, "because you've never had to fight your way through an orphanage every day. Do you think that you could fight your way past Sienne as well? Do you think I couldn't bring a dozen sailors running just by shouting?"

Angelica considered the odds. "Why even warn me?" she asked. "Why not just set that thing on me to kill me?"

That's what she would have done if she had the power to do it. If someone was a threat, you dealt with that threat. To do anything else was to leave yourself vulnerable in a world that allowed no space for such weakness.

"I'm not like you," Sophia said. "So I'm going to give you a chance, Angelica. Turn around. Walk out that door. Go back to Ashton. I won't stop you. You probably won't even see me again."

"Probably," Angelica said. Probably wasn't enough. The Dowager had been very clear about what would happen if she didn't deal with this conclusively. A traitor's death, fastened into the mask of lead while they filled it with molten metal. No, she couldn't allow that.

Nor could she allow the possibility of Sebastian finding Sophia alive at some point.

"Then I guess we have nothing more to say," Sophia said. She raised a hand, obviously ready to order her beast forward.

The key was to act without thought. Angelica shut her eyes and threw down the pouch in her hand simultaneously. Smoke and light burst from it as the impact with the floor set off the substances within. She threw herself forward, grabbing for Sophia and thrusting once, sliding the razor sharp stiletto as deep as she could get it.

She heard Sophia gasp in pain, trying to grab onto her. Angelica let the weapon go and pulled back, knowing that there would be no chance for a second thrust. She heard the forest cat roar, then saw it leap out of the smoke.

Angelica threw herself flat, feeling it pass just over the top of her. Angelica rolled to her feet, powered by fear, and lunged for the door without looking back. To look back, to slow even for a moment, was to die.

She felt claws rake across her back, burning like fire, and heard the growl of the forest cat as it attacked. She didn't stop even as she felt her flesh tear, but kept running, grabbing for the door as she went. She plunged out into the open air and slammed the door behind her, knowing that the only way to get away from the creature trying to kill her was to put a barrier in the way.

With the door shut, Angelica collapsed to the deck for a moment, putting a hand to her back. Her fingers came away wet. She forced herself back to her feet, because the noise of the fight would soon attract attention. She pushed back the way she came, making it over the side of the ship and all but falling into the small rowing boat. She gritted her teeth as she started to row, putting as much distance between her and the scene of her attack as possible.

Not attack, murder. There was no way that Sophia could survive. Even if the knife wound didn't kill her, the poison on the blade would. Angelica had done it. She'd done everything the Dowager had instructed, and she'd gotten away safely.

Now, she just had to get back to her horse and ride back to Ashton. She needed to do that with all the speed she could muster, so that she would be waiting when Sebastian got back. Was he a prize worth killing for?

No, but a kingdom might be.

CHAPTER TWENTY SIX

Sebastian pushed his stolen horse forward, racing across the countryside with as much speed as he dared in a land of hills and uneven ground. He had to get to Sophia before she left. He had to.

Already, he felt as though he was behind. He'd been trying to get to Sophia before Rupert could, but the detour he'd had to take to escape his brother's men had turned into a wider detour, until Sebastian had been so far out of his way that he had barely been able to find the way back. Now, every second that passed felt like a second in which Rupert could be hurting the woman he loved.

If he did, then Sebastian would kill him, brother or not.

The gardener, McCallum, had told him where he needed to go, so Sebastian aimed for the coast, trying to catch sight of the fishing village where the boats to Ishjemme would be. He didn't know what there was for Sophia there, and right then it didn't matter. All that mattered was that he was going to be with her.

It was one last sprint at the end of a long race to catch up with her. Sebastian still didn't know why she'd sent him the wrong way, but he hoped that it wasn't because she'd somehow stopped loving him. Sebastian wasn't sure that he could live with that, when his own love for her burned so brightly. He had to believe that she was just scared, and actually seeing him there for her would change things somehow.

"First, I have to get to her," Sebastian said, crouching low over the back of his horse to gain every hint of speed. He was back on the roads by now, because in a landscape like this, it was the only way to travel quickly, even if it meant the risk of running into Rupert and his men.

Finally, ahead, he saw the village, boats down in the harbor holding the prospect of Sophia. Sebastian could also see the uniforms of Rupert's men as they moved through the streets, obviously searching for Sophia. They were mostly at the far end of the village, but it was only a matter of time before they swept through every inch of it.

There was no time to waste, so Sebastian plunged down into the village, trying to keep low enough that Rupert and the others wouldn't see him. He tied his horse at the inn, found the door locked, and kicked it as hard as he could. On the second blow, he felt something give way, and he stumbled inside.

There were people there, staring at him in obvious terror. It took him a moment to realize that, to them, he must just look like one more of the soldiers barging through their homes. He could see a few of them with their hands under tables or hidden in cloaks, obviously getting ready to bring out weapons if they had to, but just as obviously scared of what it would mean.

"I'm not here with the others," Sebastian said. "I'm trying to find Sophia before they do."

"And why should we believe that?" a man said.

Sebastian pointed out to where Rupert was probably beating some poor person to get answers.

"That's my brother out there, and I know what he's capable of. I need to make sure that Sophia is safe. I... I love her." Sebastian knew that it was no kind of argument, but it was the only one he had.

Astonishingly, it seemed to be enough, because one of the serving girls there nodded.

"She was in here talking to Captain Borkar. His boat is the one with the seahorse figurehead."

"Thank you," Sebastian said, and ran for the harbor.

He ducked into a doorway while one of Rupert's men passed, then ran on, not wanting to stop for an instant longer than he had to. He tripped on the cobbles, forced his way back to his feet, and kept going.

The boats were just ahead, and now Sebastian found himself looking for the one with the seahorse figurehead. He was still looking around when he heard the sounds of some kind of fight ahead. Following the sound, he spotted the seahorse at the far end of the harbor, running for it as fast as he could. There was no gangplank down now, but Sebastian didn't care. He leapt, his fingers finding the rail as he pulled himself aboard.

He found himself facing a large, bearded man who stared at him as if he were an enemy to be repelled. Again, Sebastian had the sense of how he must look, and again, he didn't care. All that mattered was getting to Sophia.

"I told your master, there's no one aboard but—"

"I'm not with Rupert, and I know Sophia's here."

"Then you need to die," the big man said, reaching for a bill hook.

Sebastian hit him, not wanting to go for a weapon when it was obvious that the other man was only trying to protect Sophia. The big man stumbled, and Sebastian hit him again, sending him down to the deck. He would probably have to apologize in a while for that, but as long as he did it by Sophia's side, it didn't matter.

He looked around, trying to work out where she would be. There was a cabin toward the stern, so Sebastian headed for that. When he got to it, the door wasn't locked as he tried the handle. This was it.

"Sophia," he called out before opening it, "it's me. It's Sebastian. I'm here because… because I love you, and I want to be with you, even if that means going with you to Ishjemme and leaving my family behind. Sophia?"

There was silence from the other side of the door, and Sebastian hoped he hadn't been declaring his love to an empty room. He pushed it open, and immediately found himself faced with a creature that arched its back, hissing as it stood ready to pounce.

"It's okay," Sebastian said, using the most soothing tone he could muster as he looked around the room. "I'm not a threat."

Why anyone would keep a forest cat in a cabin, Sebastian didn't know. When the cabin appeared to be empty except for the creature, he made to shut the door again and look elsewhere on the boat for Sophia.

Then he saw the legs, just visible on the far side of the bed.

Sebastian's heart caught in his throat as he rushed forward, ignoring the forest cat for now. If that was Sophia, if the creature had hurt her…

He burst around the bed, trying to get to Sophia, trying to help her. She lay there, still and ashen, her chest not rising or falling. There was blood on her, spreading out in a pool from her chest to stain the wooden boards on which she lay.

"No," Sebastian whispered. "No."

He spun back toward the forest cat, drawing his sword, and that was when he saw the fine-bladed stiletto at the heart of the wound in Sophia's chest. Sebastian drew it out, the numbness of panic telling him that it was the first step to trying to help her. Blood oozed from the wound as he did so, and Sebastian could feel it covering his hands as he tried to hold it in by sheer force of will.

"Don't be dead," Sebastian begged, feeling tears springing into his eyes. "Please don't be dead."

Silently, he begged more than just Sophia. He prayed to the Masked Goddess, pleading and bargaining, offering his life in Sophia's place, silently cursing whoever had done this.

Mostly though, he held to Sophia and cried. If he'd loved her more, this wouldn't have happened. If he'd only ignored what she was, they could have been married by now, and safe. If he'd only gone with her when she'd left, they could have been in another place, far from the reach of this violence. Instead, he was left kneeling over her body, leaning forward to try to catch any hint of her breath, but unable to feel it against his skin.

Beside him, Sebastian heard the forest cat starting to yowl its upset, and he felt a matching howl of anguish building within him, all the pain of the things he'd lost building up until he just couldn't contain it anymore.

He cried out his pain, not caring who was listening, not caring if it brought every sailor on the ship to this cabin. What did any of it matter when the only woman he had ever loved lay there, still in a way that could only mean one thing:

Sophia was dead.

A DIRGE FOR PRINCES
(A Throne for Sisters—Book Four)

"Morgan Rice's imagination is limitless. In another series that promises to be as entertaining as the previous ones, A THRONE OF SISTERS presents us with the tale of two sisters (Sophia and Kate), orphans, fighting to survive in a cruel and demanding world of an orphanage. An instant success. I can hardly wait to put my hands on the second and third books!"

Books and Movie Reviews (Roberto Mattos)

From #1 Bestseller Morgan Rice comes an unforgettable new fantasy series.

In A DIRGE FOR PRINCES (A Throne for Sisters—Book Four), Sophia, 17, battles for her life, trying to recover from the wound left by Lady D'Angelica. Will her sister Kate's new powers be enough to bring her back?

The ship sails with the sisters to the distant and exotic lands of their uncle, their last hope and only know connection to their parents. Yet the journey is treacherous, and even if they find it, the sisters don't know if their reception will be warm or hostile.

Kate, indentured to the witch, finds herself in an increasingly desperate situation—until she meets a sorceress who may hold the secret to her freedom.

Sebastian returns to court, heartbroken, desperate to know if Sophie is alive. As his mother forces him to marry Lady D'Angelica, he knows the time has come to risk it all.

A DIRGE FOR PRINCES (A Throne for Sisters—Book Four) is the fourth book in a dazzling new fantasy series rife with love, heartbreak, tragedy, action, adventure, magic, swords, sorcery, dragons, fate and heart-pounding suspense. A page turner, it is filled with characters that will make you fall in love, and a world you will never forget.

Book #5 in the series will be released soon.

"[A THRONE FOR SISTERS is a] powerful opener to a series [that] will produce a combination of feisty protagonists and challenging circumstances to thoroughly involve not just young adults, but adult fantasy fans who seek epic stories fueled by powerful friendships and adversaries."
--Midwest Book Review (Diane Donovan)

Books by Morgan Rice

THE WAY OF STEEL
ONLY THE WORTHY (Book #1)

A THRONE FOR SISTERS
A THRONE FOR SISTERS (Book #1)
A COURT FOR THIEVES (Book #2)
A SLONG FOR ORPHANS (Book #3)
A DIRGE FOR PRINCES (Book #4)

OF CROWNS AND GLORY
SLAVE, WARRIOR, QUEEN (Book #1)
ROGUE, PRISONER, PRINCESS (Book #2)
KNIGHT, HEIR, PRINCE (Book #3)
REBEL, PAWN, KING (Book #4)
SOLDIER, BROTHER, SORCERER (Book #5)
HERO, TRAITOR, DAUGHTER (Book #6)
RULER, RIVAL, EXILE (Book #7)
VICTOR, VANQUISHED, SON (Book #8)

KINGS AND SORCERERS
RISE OF THE DRAGONS (Book #1)
RISE OF THE VALIANT (Book #2)
THE WEIGHT OF HONOR (Book #3)
A FORGE OF VALOR (Book #4)
A REALM OF SHADOWS (Book #5)
NIGHT OF THE BOLD (Book #6)

THE SORCERER'S RING
A QUEST OF HEROES (Book #1)
A MARCH OF KINGS (Book #2)
A FATE OF DRAGONS (Book #3)
A CRY OF HONOR (Book #4)
A VOW OF GLORY (Book #5)
A CHARGE OF VALOR (Book #6)
A RITE OF SWORDS (Book #7)
A GRANT OF ARMS (Book #8)
A SKY OF SPELLS (Book #9)
A SEA OF SHIELDS (Book #10)
A REIGN OF STEEL (Book #11)

About Morgan Rice

Morgan Rice is the #1 bestselling and USA Today bestselling author of the epic fantasy series THE SORCERER'S RING, comprising seventeen books; of the #1 bestselling series THE VAMPIRE JOURNALS, comprising twelve books; of the #1 bestselling series THE SURVIVAL TRILOGY, a post-apocalyptic thriller comprising three books; of the epic fantasy series KINGS AND SORCERERS, comprising six books; of the epic fantasy series OF CROWNS AND GLORY, comprising 8 books; and of the new epic fantasy series A THRONE FOR SISTERS. Morgan's books are available in audio and print editions, and translations are available in over 25 languages.

Morgan loves to hear from you, so please feel free to visit www.morganricebooks.com to join the email list, receive a free book, receive free giveaways, download the free app, get the latest exclusive news, connect on Facebook and Twitter, and stay in touch!

Made in the USA
San Bernardino, CA
30 January 2018